Between Eden and the Open Road

PHILIP GABER

DEDICATION

This book is for those to whom it speaks

Table of Contents

she's alone but chemically balanced

See her there. Looking very ill-at-ease. Don't know why. Maybe because she isn't happy with her makeup. Maybe because she's menstruating. Maybe because she just doesn't feel like being friendly. It's like she believes in something beyond her experience, but is afraid to commit to it. She likes to project herself onto people who are monotonous. Always becomes impatient with clichés and hackneyed plots. She doesn't understand why it rains or why there's lightning in the sky or how many senators there are, but she knows how to manipulate a man, for damn sure, and how to suspend belief, which is always a valuable skill to have. So what if her boyfriend thinks she's "certifiably coo coo?" She still has nice firm tits and a face that adolescent boys fantasize about.

She looks in the mirror. Time to lose the glasses and get Lasik surgery.

Looks at the bags under her eyes and the crow's feet. Time for a little plastic surgery.

Lifts her blouse, looks at her belly. Time for liposuction.

Her hair is still blonde, there's no sign of any graying. Done everything wrong my whole life, she thinks, and still have enough residual confidence left over to... It's no good. The thought is no good; mostly because she can't complete it. She is forever beginning thoughts and not finishing them. She chalks this up to having recently diagnosed herself with Adult Attention Deficit Disorder after watching a commercial on the Lifetime network. Or was it Oxygen? She can never keep those two networks straight. All she knows is one of them used to play reruns of Oprah and the other... oh, who the hell knows... the wine is the thing... and the third glass is really the thing...

In her journal that night she writes:

"I would have been called voguish in the twenties, reactionary in the thirties, cantankerous in the forties, obstreperous in the fifties, liverish in the sixties, nebulous in the seventies, self-denying in the eighties, semi-conscious in the nineties... these days I'm just called a laughing sinner... I've really scrambled to get where I am... I'm common... a proletariat...

my lips have become a joke... my eyebrows, exaggerated... my eyes, presbyopic... my vocabulary, tiresome... don't even know the definition of "self." I'm plucky, but disengaged, slavishly devoted to feather-light comedies... I aggressively seek out the role of being on the down-low... I have an arsenal of rage..."

She puts the pen down, closes her eyes and thinks about something her mother once said to her: "The secret is being able to do anything and not knowing where you're going to end up at the end of the day and just letting fate fall into the palm of your hand."

She looks carefully at the palms of her hands. They're the only parts of me that have not aged, she thinks, and she sighs.

nothing but real

She was in her chair, secured, sedated, colorless.

"This whole thing seems small,"
she said softly with her breath,
then showed me the creases in her elbows.
"Heat rash… itches…"

I smiled at her.

"Your teeth are not that straight," she said.
"Not too white, either…
Don't you think you'd feel a whole lot better
with straighter, whiter teeth?"

I shook my head.

"Why not?" she said.

"I'm not that interested in my teeth," I said.

"I had an uncle that never brushed his teeth," she said.
"Doctor said plaque got into his bloodstream,
causing him to have a stroke… You believe that?"

"Anything's possible," I said.

She stared at the wall for about five minutes,
then fell off to sleep,
holding the geegaw someone had given her
to help her remind her of her personality.

When I left the ward,
I crossed the street,
went into an ill-lit barrelhouse, and sat
in the corner under a photograph of
a smiling, toothless hermit.

A short, narrow-eyed woman with a

soft-lined face approached me.

"What can I get for you tonight, sweetie?" she said.

"A gin sling," I said.

"Haven't had anybody order a
gin sling in years," she said.
"What's the occasion?"

I looked up at the smiling hermit,
then at the woman.

"Just trying to glue someone back together," I said

The waitress nodded
as if she understood completely.

"Well, good luck with that," she said, and left.

I glanced at the photograph
one last time and
resolved to standby her
through all of her hallucinations.

melancholy jew

He was the Monday morning of human beings.

The kind of guy who would confront you
in a public rest room if you
didn't wash your hands
or shooed you with his fingers and bellowed,
"C'mon, c'mon!"
the second the stop light changed from
red to green.

In the late afternoon, he started drinking
Machiavellian martinis
and by about 7:30
he'd become vaguely hostile.

If you asked him a question,
he purposely muttered something inaudible.

If you asked him to repeat himself,
he snapped at you and asked to be left alone
and then wallowed in a kind of
emotional reaction to either good or bad
memories for the rest of the night.

Once during a Passover Seder,
with the entire family present,
he stood up as if he were going
to propose a toast and said:

"Jesus Christ,
with all the fardreyen kopf and shadenfreuding
goin' on in this family,
is it any wonder why we're so
estranged from one another?"

Then, gulping the last of his

Manischewitz Concord grape wine,
he stormed out,
taking the afikomen with him.

from my own weight

It's about not returning the smiles
of others or mirroring their enthusiasm.

It's about not extending myself.

It's about refraining from competition and
scorning those who revel in it.

It's about loneliness and being
too involved in my own head.

It's about only seeing the
ugliness in others and in me.

It's about distortions and exaggerations.

It's about my broken heart and doubling-up on
the floor after a thousand self-incriminations and
a thousand and one reasons why I'm a failure.

It's about writing the same thing over and over.

It's about other people's judgments and
criticisms and how they shape my
self-perception, my self-esteem, my reality.

It's about despising and envying the optimism in others.

It's about alienating myself from my family and
running away from those who care for me and love me.

It's about being ashamed to discuss my pain with others.

It's about thinking that if people knew
the real me they would be disappointed.

It's about drifting.

It's about walking in a fog for forty odd years
of my life without knowing exactly what it is
I should be doing or which goals I should be
setting or what job I should be applying for or
what woman I should be spending
the rest of my life with.

It's about missed opportunities and not hustling enough.

It's about resignation, anxiety, self-consciousness,
introversion, selfishness, isolation, indifference,
detachment, anger, bitterness, petulance, immaturity,
arrogance, pride, sloth, lust.

It's about yearning to belong and a craving for privacy.

It's about contradictions and ironies,
conflicts and harmonies,
warring with my demons,
and making peace with myself.

It's about being embarrassed to show
my emotions, especially enthusiasm and
joy and tenderness and the belief that
anger is the only emotion I'm permitted to express.

It's about cynicism and paranoia,
a lack of trust and an abundance of blame.

It's about denial and self-loathing.

It's about self-deprecation and modesty.

It's about deference and reticence.

It's about a loss of language and
articulating my anger with silence.

the trauma caused me to retract

Drinking my wine a little too fast, it suddenly occurred to me that I was alone, spiritually bankrupt and without anything to eat. Not only that, the woman I was dating at that second was feeding me lines like: "You're such a man of consequence," and "I've never met anyone with such extraneous values."

Determined to cheer myself up, I opened a chapbook of poetry entitled "Expunging the Inner Adult", by Bartholomew Cobbler, and came across a poem titled,

"Break a Lovely Pill In Half in Her Coffee

She was last seen
knees to her chest
arms hugging her shins
rocking to and fro
mumbling,
'Somebody heal me, somebody heal me…'"

I flipped the page and read another one.

"God I'm Tired

It was cold out.
Just about dusk dark.
The moon looked like open-heart surgery.
Her hand reminded me of broken glass.
Her relapse was like a sinking ship
in the Nevada desert.

Her soul was walking around in
bedroom slippers mumbling,
'Peace and forgiveness were denied me on this earth…
let us pray.'"

I was beginning to get the hang of old Bartholomew. He really knew his way around the English language. I think he was making a conscious effort to…*do* something…make the reader *feel* something…incomplete, ephemeral, alone? Make them aware of their existential pain? And what about that last poem?

"Plump & Schvitzing

I
draw
the
line
at
swamis."

Only 6 words, but ohh the brevity. So terse and lean, incorruptible, uncompromising.

And then the phone rang. It was my lady.

"You're not drinking alone again, are you?" she said.

"Absolutely not," I said.

"What are you doing?"

"Reading some poems."

"Wow, a sensitive guy. That's encouraging. I should warn you up front I'm a sexual predator."

Several seconds went by, then she laughed. "I told you about my sense of humor in my email," she said.

"Yes, you did."

"You didn't laugh."

"I smiled inside."

She sighed. "Ohhh I do enjoy your humanity on a certain level."

"Thanks."

"So what are those poems about?"

"They're transitory in nature."

"God, I love the way you break things down to their most basic fundamental concept. Read me one."

I turned to the table of contents and looked for a provocative title.

"Shooting to Death's Door

I was living a heightened reality,
a lyrical reality.
Nobody understood what my rhythms
were all about.
It became an ego thing.
I wasn't a good bet, health-wise
but I still allowed myself to be seen.
I reinvented myself, mainly, to try
and get people to see me.
If they would have just allowed me to
be myself,
it would have been a lot different."

I waited for her response.

"Done?" she said.

"Yes."

"Well..."

"What do you think?"

"I don't like it."

"Why not?"

"It's pretentious. It tries too hard to be... profound. Don't you think so?"

"I like it."

"What do you like about it?"

"It's unrelenting. It provokes me."

"To do what?"

"Think"

"Well, whatever. I'm tired of thinking. I gotta go. I'll talk to you later."

I hung up the phone, turned to page 123, read the first few lines:

"Endings Mean Never Having to Say I Love You

I didn't believe in romantic love.
And on the other hand, I kept falling in love.
Tears would shoot out of my face
whenever I met somebody."

I closed the chapbook and thought; love is one of the few mysteries we can
still count on.

the energy of nothing

We didn't possess a lot of insight,
just a lot of adolescent myopia.

We were more metaphysical than our elders
gave us credit for.

We embodied something,
though we could never put it
into an essay,
for example,
or a letter-to-the-editor.

We held beliefs,
which was unusual for a generation
bereft of a mission statement.

We believed in the
power of neurosis and
weren't ashamed of flaunting
our talent for posing the
philosophical issues
of life and death and
having no answers.

We weren't searchers,
although we were self-taught,
to some degree.

College was never an option.

Options were never an option.

We maybe went to community college
for twelve and a half minutes or
got an internship at a
classic rock radio station
or went to work for a

wedding photographer
as a videographer's gofer,
but most of our days were spent
smoking reefer in the back of
somebody's El Camino,
listening to Pink Floyd's "The Wall",
reminiscing about all the chicks
we wished we'd bagged in high school.

We never had a Defining Moment,
never came to any epiphanies,
held devilish anger inside of us,
but were graced with instincts of godhood.

We were alive with the
eye of the tiger syndrome and
became something of an
unsolved puzzle to social workers
who couldn't wait to drop us
from their caseloads.

Then one day we just sort of started
settling for less
than those who didn't even
have the opportunity to
negotiate for more,
while everyone else
had tomorrows to burn.

comfort

The joke in those days was that Muriel Fink wasn't sexy, just alive. Very few people ever laughed at that joke.

To their credit.

One night a priest caught her tying a necktie around her elbow.

"What are you doing that for?" he asked her.

"Gotta 40 pound monkey climbing up my back, Father," she told him.

"A monkey?"

"Yessir."

When she took a hypodermic needle from her purse, the priest's eyes suddenly gained weight. "Mary, Joseph and…" He moistened his lips. "What on earth are you…" He swallowed hard. Sore throat hard. "Please tell me you're a diabetic," he said.

Muriel stuck the needle in her arm. "Hardly, Father," she said, closing her eyes. Her head fell forward. Her chin rested on her chest. "I'm just about habitual… I tried to give it a chance… tried to go on and on and on… but I owe too much… I'm just too much in debt…"

"In debt to what? To whom?" the priest said.

Muriel tossed the needle into the trash can and put on a raincoat, the kind the Morton salt girl used to wear. "You name it," she said.

The priest sighed. Poured a scotch straight up. Loosened his collar with his index finger. Perspiration sneaked out of every pour in his skin. "I'm…" He paused. "I…" He could no longer look Muriel in the eye. "I was under the impression that you had…" He took an aggressive pull of Chivas. "…More self control…"

Muriel rested her head against the back of the chair. Smiled unselfconsciously. And slightly seductively. "Father, is it a sin to say I want to run away?"

"What are you running away from?"

Muriel clucked her tongue. "Treachery…fraud…apostasy…"

The priest took a deep Far Eastern breath. Nodded compassionately. "We are all faced with the temptation of running away," he said. "I have often fantasized about running away from the Church." He stroked his collar. "But what good would it do? What would it solve? What would God think of me if I just… ran away?" He paused. "He'd be very disappointed in me, wouldn't He?"

Muriel stared at the palms of her hands and nodded. Quietly. "Do you think He'd be disappointed in me if I ran away?" she said.

The priest swallowed soft. Ice-cream soft. "Yes, He'd be very disappointed…and so would I…"

The muscles in Muriel's face twitched. "What am I going to do?" she said.

"You can begin by forgiving yourself," the priest said. "…loving yourself… being yourself…"

Muriel retrieved a silver cigarette case from her purse. Opened it. Fingered a Thai stick. "You know you're talking to a Jewish girl, Father…"

The priest smiled. "We're all God's children…"

Muriel nodded. "I kind of expected you to say something like that," she said, lighting the Thai stick with a Bic Banana and taking a long toke. As she blew the smoke out of the side of her mouth, she said, "Want some? You can pretend it's incense…"

The priest stood up. Awkwardly. "I'll pray for you," he said.

"Thank you, Father…I depend on the kindness of clergymen…"

As the priest walked to the door, Muriel said, "Father, are you sure I can't run away?"

The priest turned to face Muriel one last time. Said, "You have my blessing," and was gone before Muriel could drift off into another daydream about purgatory.

serious freedom

Blew into town like a reputable vagrant,
with a pack of smokes and a
full flask of apple jack and a
quarter of a chip still left
on my shoulder.

I checked my watch.

It had stopped.

Checked the sun.

It was a few minutes fast.

Ducked into a movie theater.

A film by Jolly Johns was showing,
starring somebody named Roxie Fuller.
She was chronically dissatisfied
with something,
something intangible,
inscrutable.
Kept chain smoking and
picking up guys at a bar
in a Holiday Inn.
Wore lots of lip gloss and
purple eye shadow and high heels
that made her wobble like a Weeble.

I walked out an eighth of the way
through the movie,
(had nobody to root for),
was accosted by a woman whose face
was scarred by acne.
She bummed a cigarette from me,
asked me if I could ever vote for
somebody who was pro-life.

Told her, I don't vote.

She said why not.

Told her, don't complain
so I don't vote.

She said, well at least you're consistent.

Told her, that I am, sister,
that I am,
excused myself,
walked east,
or was it west?

Definitely wasn't north or south.

Could've been northeast or southeast.

Decided it really didn't matter
because I was a reputable vagrant
with a quarter of a chip still left
on my shoulder,
goodly in need of a crucial moment and
black coffee,
secretly yearning
for precise reasoning and
a Pop tart,
but settling for
the middle ground and
something 3 weeks past
its expiration date.

something just short of disheveled

I moved around,
here and there,
sold mantras on the street
for a buck seventy-five apiece,
tried to become mainstream
but the counterculture wasn't having it.

They kidnapped me,
threw me in the back of a Volkswagen bus,
fed me cheap wine from a brown jug,
pumpkin seeds and sunflower seeds
in honey,
read from Das Kapital,
Allen Ginsberg,
made me audition for the role of
Claude Hooper Bukowski
in a road production of "Hair".

I wasn't feeling their
rhetoric or their sideburns,
so I escaped and landed on my knees
next to some stray cats
who were waiting on their
SSI benefits.

I ducked into a bookstore
owned by a man in a red baseball cap
and a Santa Claus beard.

He nearly blinded me with
his high-beam eyes and offered
me a cup of green tea.

"You look like you could use a friend
and some meaningful conversation," he said.

I nodded,

even though I was too sleepy
for friendship or meaningful conversation.

I asked him if he had a back room where
I could take a nap for about
an hour or so.

"You ain't a narc, are ya?" he said.

"No, sir."

He pointed to a door in the rear
of the store that a had a cardboard sign
thumb-nailed to it:

GOING HOME,
it said, and it looked like
it was painted with
fluorescent red spray paint.

I turned the knob to the right
but it was locked.

I turned it to the left and it opened.

I looked back at the owner,
who was binding a copy of the
King James Bible,
smoking Indian bidis and watching
cartoons on a 13-inch black and white TV.

I entered the room.

It looked to be about 9 by 12.

There was a cot leaning against the
far wall.

I lay down and took a few deep breaths.

My nose began to run.

There was a powerful odor of eucalyptus
in the air.

I closed my eyes.

I heard some voices on the other side
of the wall.

Two young men,
probably teenagers,
skipping school.

- I dunno, man…

- Dude, you're sweating…

- Yeah, my heart's goin' crazy, too…I'm not gonna do anymore…

- It's not cut right…something's off…

- Yeah, flush it down the shitter…I ain't in the mood to OD tonight…

When I awoke, the sun was just coming up.

And I became half a human being again,
in and of myself.

very lutheran and very agonized

The music coming from my trumpet was sarcastic and tongue-in-cheek. It had been ever since Sheila, the woman I'd been dating for seven years, had ended our relationship by mailing me a two-line letter from Kissimmee that said:

"Sometimes silence is also an answer...I am, after all, very Lutheran and very agonized...Sheila."

I recalled her shell of seeming indifference, the nightmares she used to talk about at the breakfast table, her love of black Renault sedans, bialys, frog's legs, Wild Turkey and cheap motels.

And nobody could interpret nonverbal communication better than Sheila.

"Eyebrows lie," she once told me. "So do upper lips and cheeks. Chins and earlobes are pretty much straight-shooters."

As I emptied the spit valve on my horn, the phone rang.

It was Sheila calling from Kissimmee.

"You know I've been badly damaged by the world and that I'm a woman of excess and failure," she said.

"Join the club," I said.

"Always a cigarette in one hand and a glass of bourbon in the other... and I'm an ergophobe."

"A what?"

"I have a fear of work."

"I'm aware of that."

Long pause.

"Anyway," she said. "Chin up."

"Chin up?"

"You'll be alright."

"What about you?"

"I'll be alright, too. Just gotta stay away from drama and decadence, you know what I mean, jellybean?"

"No."

"Me neither. But I can front with the best of 'em. Toodaloo, bugaboo!"

"Wait a minute-"

"Gotta go, man. Gonna donate some of my eggs."

"What?"

"This fertility clinic. They're payin' like 2 g's for eggs. Mama's got rent to pay."

"Don't do that. I can loan you… whatever you need…"

"Dominus vobiscum, dude!"

"Whaa?"

"Gotta go!"

"Sheila?!"

Click.

Dial tone.

I went back into the bathroom to take a leak.

After zipping up, I peered into the mirror.

"I don't love Sheila. I don't love Sheila. I don't love Sheila."

My eyebrows appeared noncommittal, however, my cheeks and upper lip seemed to be in denial.

I picked up my horn and played taps, this time with very little rancor.

trying to sleep the sleep of the just

It was our first date. She was on her fourth cosmopolitan. I was sipping some oak-softened, full-bodied house wine.

"See, now, you're an introvert," she said. "You don't give a fuck, excuse my French, about people. You're not out there playing kissy-kissy with everybody, you don't have time for that shit. Everything's internal with you," she tapped on her chest several times. "You live up here," she pointed to her temple. "But there's nothing wrong with that. That's *you*. Everybody's different. And the reason people are comfortable around you, you're safe. You don't rock boats, you keep to yourself, you're not gonna get all up in people's faces and challenge them 'cuz you don't have time for that shit! You could care less! I know. My son's an introvert. And, I think, introverted men have a much harder time of it socially. And in the business world. Much harder than women. Most introverted men I know are pretty much," she shrugged. "insufficient... I don't know how else to say it."

That's when I began to feel nauseous.

She described her last boyfriend as "an enormous dominant male," her parents as "downwind, out of sight and full of impatience," her siblings as "wandering visibly about," her friends as "more greedy than deadly," and herself as "beyond help and hope."

By the time the check arrived, we decided to split it, because I was having trouble staying awake and she was through emasculating me.

As we drove home, she said, "I kind of wish I could rewind my life and do it all over again. There's a lot of things I would have done differently."

I nodded.

"Are you mad at me?" she said.

"No..."

"You know why I wore pink tonight?"

"Why?"

"Pink is the color of divine love."

"I didn't know that," I said.

She stared out the window. "I'm tired of dividing my affection between sex and love. Between life and death. I hope the next time we speak can be a whole lot more jovial."

When we turned into her apartment complex, I pulled into the only vacant parking space in front of her building.

She got out of the car, didn't say goodbye, just slammed the door and walked toward her apartment.

I probably should have waited until she was safely inside before I drove away, but I didn't. I couldn't throw the car in reverse fast enough.

The next day, there was a message from her on my answering machine:

"I don't know, I feel bad, almost. You know what I'm saying. Like I kind of feel, like, just like, oh my God, this... I'm this poor little girl that might have some serious issues I might not be ready to face."

There was about thirty seconds of dead air before she resumed her self-analysis.

"I think I can drink and use my drinking as an excuse to possibly let out my real self sometimes."

More dead air.

"When I have alcohol in me, it's different...so is that the alcohol or is that me? I don't understand."

It's you, baby.

"Well," she continued. "We probably shouldn't see each other again. I guess I'll leave that up to you. Vaya con Dios, hombre, que sera sera, mas o menos..."

I deleted her message and went to bed.

the ballad of all i know

I

The phone would ring.

"Hello," I'd say.

"You said you were gonna call me."

It was always Heidi,
a girl I'd met at an
adult children of alcoholics/dysfunctional
families support group.

She always wore black because
she thought black was sexy.
but the way she wore black
it was like she was in mourning.

"You got company?" she'd say.

"No," I'd say, and whoever was in my bed
would look at me funny.

"I've had a change of heart," Heidi would say. "I want you to move in
with me..."

"Oh, really?"

"You're the only one who gets me."

I'd usually go silent on purpose at that point.

"Oh so, you don't love me, anymore?" she'd say.

"I didn't say that," I'd say.

"You didn't have to."

"Why do you say that?"

"Because you're in bed with some chick right now
who's trying to figure you out."

I'd just close my eyes,
take a deep breath and pray for a simpler life.

"It's too bad," she'd say.
"We could have had a little
somethin'-somethin' together,"
and she'd hang up and I wouldn't hear from her
again for at least two or three days.

I'd climb back into bed and whomever
was lying there would say,
"Who was that?"
and I'd shake my head and sigh and say, "Don't worry about it."

"It's another woman."

"No one like you,"
which never seemed to satisfy them.
Only made them more competitive and bitchy.

"She ain't got nothin' on me," they'd say,
and I'd agree with them and close my eyes
and fall asleep with their arms around me.

II

I'd wake up and it would always
be raining and my sunglasses could never
keep the glare of her honesty from blinding me.

She'd say, "So now what's your plan?"

I'd hem and haw and do what slackers usually do,
crack a Pabst Blue Ribbon and smoke a bowl.
Then I'd say something like,
"Well, the thing of it is…" and nothing more.

Had no plan.

Never did.

Most I ever had was a fragment of a plan,
a fragmented fragment of a plan.

I'd lived my whole life like that.

Always fucked up with women
during the most crucial point in our
intercourse.

Always dropped the ball with them.

Never knew how to answer them,
always felt like I was on a job interview,
whether we were eating dinner or in
post coital cool-down,
they were always trying to
get inside my ambition,
wanting to know if I had
anything to offer them,
the world,
their family.

We'd be lying there,
sweaty,
out of breath,
smelling of semen and vaginal juices,
staring at the missing tiles in the ceiling.

They'd be asking me questions, boy.

"Want children?"

"Dunno."

"Wanna get married?"

"Dunno."

"Wanna better job?"

"Dunno."

Then there'd be like 3 minutes of silence.

They'd be thinking,
This guy seems like one of those
conflicted guys who never seems to be able
to form attachments with women.

I'd be thinking,
Jesus Christ, now what?

a night of profound love

I was looking for healing, so I drove to a house of ill-repute.

When I arrived, the madam took me by the hand and asked me to repent for my sins, but I wasn't in any mood for repentance; it was the Sabbath and I'd recently recovered from a bout of bacterial gastroenteritis. As she lit an opium-laced bidi, she told me a fairy tale about grief and loss. When the curtain finally fell on the third act of her story, she was laughing but I was in tears.

I was about to excuse myself when an up-and-coming ingénue appeared. She was pale and frail, had a G-rated walk and an X-rated face.

The madam (she was really a madwoman) introduced us.

"Lolita, I'd like you to meet…"

"Boris," I lied.

I could feel Lolita sizing me up. Her eyes focused on my package for about two and a half seconds. Not that I'm bragging.

"How long have you been alone?" Lolita said.

I swallowed with some difficulty, felt my Adam's apple bobbing and my nervous system short circuiting. "Alone?" I said.

"Looks to me like you need a little lovin' in your heart," she said, smiling like a woman alive in the line of duty.

My first impulse was to run away, (that always seems to be my first impulse whenever I'm confronted by a strong woman), but I maintained eye contact, even managed to smile, (although my erection subsided).

"Do you enjoy your work?" I said.

Lolita looked at the madam, who rolled her eyes and pursed her lips.

"We don't typically describe our line of work as being enjoyable," the madam said. "But it sure beats the hell out of bein' an admin assistant."

They both laughed. It was one of those two-fold laughs; designed to completely humiliate me and stop me from saying anything else.

"If it's a hiding place you want," Lolita said. "I think I can provide you with a shroud of privacy."

"Or perhaps you like the zaftig, chatty type," the madam said, signaling for one of the other girls.

"Actually, uhh," I said.

"Oh, don't worry," the madam said. "She's as gentle as rain."

"I really should go," I said. "I've had this bacterial gastroenteritis thing and…"

"Ursula!" croaked the madam.

Just then, a wasp-waisted qualmish femme fatale entered the room. "Ursula's still exfoliating quiet hysteria from her pores," she said to the madam; then she looked at me. "Perhaps I can quell your hunger."

"This is Adrianna," the madam said with a smirk. "She says she was put here on earth to enable the divine unfolding of the universe."

"Well," Adrianna said. "My word is all I have."

Lolita rolled her eyes, sat down, got on her cell phone and ordered a refill of liquid Valium.

"Well, I'll leave you two alone," the madam said and left the room.

Adrianna approached me, wiping allergies from her eyes. "I don't want you to be intimidated around me because I realize, like, I project that all the time."

"I'm not." I said. "I'm just trying to acclimate myself to my surroundings."

"Mmm. A man of letters."

"Not really. I was in prison. I read the dictionary a lot."

"What did you do?"

"Grand theft and vandalism."

"Excuse me?"

"I stole a koi fish from a Japanese restaurant, barbequed it, and ate it."

"Hunh…"

"It was a fraternity prank. Spent a year in the county jail."

"Interesting."

"I think the district attorney was just trying to make a name for him in order to position himself for the state senate, so he prosecuted me."

"A real life felon. That's a turn on."

"Misdemeanor."

"Ahh-hah."

That's when her beeper sounded. As soon as she realized who was beeping her, she practically began to hyperventilate.

"Oh my God. Oh my God! Oh my God oh my God! *Habib!* It's *Habib!*"

"Who's Habib?"

"He's an African prince, from the Republic of Congo. Well, he says he's a prince. I think he's just using that as an angle, but he is loaded. And he loves white women. And he's gotta huge…Well, you don't wanna hear that. Anyway, it was great to meet you!"

"Same here."

Adrianna began gathering her belongings. "I really wanna hear more about your time in the county jail," she said. "I hear such horror stories. Must've been awful…"

"It was mostly a question of holding onto the soap, really," I said.

She laughed. "Oh, that's funny… Well, bye!" And she left.

That's when my nausea subsided.

As I walked out the door, I noticed an aging drag queen standing in the shadows, checking her makeup in a compact, affirming herself. "Beautiful white bitch born to drive men wild."

I got in my car and headed for Goldenrod Kisses in York Beach.

It had been years since I'd had a decent piece of taffy.

quiet

I don't know why I don't
have anything to say.

Maybe it's because I've
resigned myself
to those pedestrian silences.

out of panic comes laughter

It's quiet today.

I'm sitting under the big apple tree
in the back yard,
but I'm tired for some reason.

I tell myself I'm not going to drink
today and I don't,
but I want to.

Badly.

My cell phone rings.

It's my brother Joey.

He wants to know if I'm coming
for the holidays this year.

I tell him I'm not sure.
It depends on a few things.

"What things?" he asks.

"Joey," I say.
"I'm just too tired for specifics
at the moment.
You're just gonna have to accept that."

He's offended.
Says, "Well, it wouldn't hurt you
to get up off of that couch for a change."

I tell him it would be nice to spend
the holidays with him and his bi-polar wife.

He explodes,
"YOU ASSHOLE! WHY DON'T YOU SEEK THERAPY?"

I snicker,
loudly enough for him to hear.

He is not pleased with me.

I don't blame him.

I want to hang up on him but I don't.

I can hear him hyperventilating.

He just got picked up with
high blood pressure and he's really
trying to control his emotions.

He covers the mouthpiece with his hand,
says something to his bi-polar wife,
then uncups the mouthpiece, and says, "You working?"

"Yes, Joey," I say.
"I'm working," and
wait for the follow-up.

"Where you working?"

"I am currently working as a collections specialist."

"A what?"

"You know what collections are, don't you?"

"Yes."

"Well, I am a collections specialist.
 I specialize in collections."

"Alright, alright," he says.

"I'm just telling you what I do for a living, Joey."

"Fine…"

"It's really not that bad.
I'm actually enjoying it.
I feel bad for some of these people.
Some of their stories are just heartbreaking."

There's a pause.

Then Joey says, "Right, right, I can imagine…
So can we plan on you being here?"

"Sure, Joey. Providing I can finagle
a little time off from my j-o-b,
I'd be delighted to attend."

"Well, let us know."

"I will do that."

"Take care of yourself."

"Thank you."

He hangs up.

I turn my phone off and continue
tearing up my old childhood pictures.

the tension, the existence

I wake up at four in the morning sweating all over the sheets, teary-eyed, nauseous, burning sensation in my chest.

The only sounds, the leak in the shower head dripping into the tub, the buzzing refrigerator, and a not-so-distant train whistle.

I cough, belch, feel a sneeze gaining momentum in my nasal cavity, but my mucous membranes have decided they aren't irritated enough, and so the sneeze withdraws, temporarily.

I lie in bed, waiting for that paralyzing sleep, as the drip drip drip from the shower head reminds me of all those World War II B-movies where the Japanese tortured our POW's by dripping water onto their foreheads.

Drip drip drip.

I hear the guy upstairs moving around.

I can even hear him pissing into his toilet; you really know you're living in a cheap piece of crap apartment when you can hear the guy above you pissing into the toilet.

He flushes.

He might as well be flushing my toilet, that's how loud it is.

He turns on his TV; another poor bastard kept awake by the mocking voices in his head.

I try sleeping on my right side, my left side, on my back, flat on my stomach, left side, right side, fetal position, two pillows, three pillows, no pillows, one pillow stuffed between my legs, covers kicked to the foot of the bed, just a sheet and a blanket, two blankets over my head, under my chin, under my arm. Why are my arms always in the way whenever I'm trying to sleep?

The guy upstairs has got the blender going.

Margaritas at five in the morning? A milkshake? What the hell could he be pureeing at this hour of the fucking morning?

Oh, good, now the birds are awake.

Is that a woodpecker?

Sounds like a drum roll on bark.

And now the guy upstairs has decided that at five thirty in the morning, his carpet needs a going over with the vacuum.

Christ, with that kind of suction power, he ought to be able to suck the dirt right out of my carpet, too.

Deep breaths.

They say if you close your eyes and take deep breaths, it'll help you get to sleep.

In through the nose, out through the mouth, in through the nose, out through the mouth.

Ohh now the cockapoo next door is whimpering for her breakfast, that's nice.

And somebody on the other side of my bedroom wall is doing jumping jacks or calisthenics or Zumba and suddenly people are rising and shining and taking showers and flushing toilets and making breakfast and opening and closing cabinets and drawers and closet doors and medicine cabinets and locking their front doors and walking down three, four, five, six flights of stairs in high heels and steel-toed boots and opening and slamming car doors, and igniting their cars, sometimes two or three times before the engine finally turns over.

Tires are squealing and crawling across loose gravel and garbage trucks are lifting dumpsters and emptying them of their refuse.

Later that day the manager of my apartment complex leaves a message on my answering machine.

"Somebody reported a disturbance coming from your area last night. Said there was some dancing or jumping around going on. A television apparently was being played loudly as well as some very aggressive vacuuming? If you know anything about this, please give us a call at your earliest convenience and thank you for your cooperation."

a rough full-contact love

I always seem to be craning my neck
in order to get a better view of life.

I always seem to be motioning my fingers
toward a destination unknown.

I always seem to be sticking out my tongue
in the middle of snowstorms whenever I
have a fever in order to lower my
body temperature by a couple of degrees.

I always seem to be hooking opposing index fingers
into the corners of my mouth
in an attempt to stretch my
cheeks beyond their limit.

I always seem to be on the verge of
something terrific like becoming employed again.

I always seem to be thinking up new ways of kissing;
I've perfected a technique whereby I follow through
by brushing up against your incisors with my
lower lip and flicking the nerve linked to your
throat muscle with the tip of my tongue.

I always seem to be mentioning your name
in mixed company while I'm in the middle
of introducing myself to strangers.

I always seem to be power walking
on tightropes made of egg shells
whenever I'm beating off around your bush.

I always seem to be going this-a-way,
that-a-way, and ending up in Piscataway and
I always seem to be able
to stop my love on a dime.

some equilibrium between writing and living

I

They're sitting together on the couch watching some epic tragedy about obsession and discovery on Lifetime when he suddenly gets that queasy feeling in the pit of his stomach and excuses himself.

"Going to bed," he says. "Tired."

"It's only seven o'clock," she says.

"Mm, I know."

II

He drinks some gin, walks outside, smokes a cigarette, stares at the sky, and tries to remember one thing he learned about stars from science class, but can only recall something about them being big balls of plasma.

Then, feeling a chill near his shoulder bones, he goes into his bedroom, sits down at the old portable manual typewriter, writes about autumn roses and winter twilights as metaphors for the blocks and impasses that sometimes impairs his life, becomes impatient with its lack of intrinsic drama, rips the paper from the typewriter carriage, and tosses it over his shoulder.

III

Looking out into the heavy night, he drinks more gin, smokes another cigarette, mutters, "What's wrong with me," wonders when he will give up this pretentious role of asking the immortal questions.

And then this memory:

Living in New York in a basement room. Sitting naked in a broken arm chair, drinking straight Scotch, unable to sleep, reading something by Robert Penn Warren.

"When you get born your father and mother lost something out of themselves, and they are going to bust a hame trying to get it back, and you are it. They know they can't get it all back but they will get as big a chunk out of you as they can. And the good old family reunion, with picnic dinner under the maples, is very much like diving into the octopus at the aquarium."

Going home that weekend, his father, soaked in bourbon and weepy from some deep sorrow, admits that he was an accident and begged his mother to abort him.

IV

After threading another sheet of paper into the typewriter's carriage, he types, "There's a chill of solitude in the air," and he shivers.

Have I lost the art of being alone? he thinks.

V

He wakes the following morning and wanders into the kitchen, makes a pot of coffee, sits in the breakfast nook, reads the headline above the fold in the newspaper.

Complicated, Opaque, Contradictory and Subtle Man Awakes

LIMBO (AP) — The outlook was uncertain today as he awoke to find the content of his life story had neither arc nor theme, no narrative trajectory and no central idea.

VI

"You were up late," she says, joining him.

"Mmm…"

"Get a lot done?"

He waits before answering. "Never that far away from a Pulitzer," he says, pouring another cup of coffee.

And never that far away from going too deeply inside my mind, he thinks. God knows there's a lot of room there.

the bright coming morn

The other day I met a tramp in a sober suit.

He was drunk.

And complaining that the sun was in his eyes.

"Don't mind sun," he said. "'Cept when it's in my eyes," and he took out a pair of cheap sunglasses, the kind ZZ Top sang about, and put them on.

He looked like a blind man with those sunglasses on.

I know that sounds ridiculous, but he did.

He was about five feet four inches tall and must have weighed about a hundred and thirty pounds. He had a lot of alcohol swimming inside of him. I imagined the alcohol doing the butterfly or the breast stroke or maybe even the backstroke.

He was what my mammy called "booze-sodden."

So booze-sodden, that I began to feel like I was getting a contact drunk from the guy.

"Do you mind if I read something to you?" said the tramp.

"No, sir," I said.

He took out one of those Moleskin pocket notebooks; the kind they say Hemingway used.

I wondered if that was the reason he bought the notebook.

I was about to ask him that very question when he began to speak: "You know, they say Hemingway used a notebook just like this. 'Course, I had no idea until the sales clerk told me so." I've found if you wait around long enough, people will usually answer most of your questions for you without you ever having to ask them. The tramp opened the book and began reading. "...and then the sun shone, blinding me to the possibilities of the light, and some young, beautiful, eclectic girl with a great personality whispered, it's amazing how good I feel when the sun is out, and came home with me and fellated me in a way that no other young, beautiful, eclectic girl with a great personality had ever fellated me before... and I was happy... for the moment... because, as you know, (or may not know, depending on your level of knowing), happiness is a fickle mistress who sometimes likes to falsely accuse you of communicating threats... and that is when the matter must then be resolved in small claims court, preferably adjudicated by somebody who passed a bar on the way over to the courthouse...which is about the time I looked at my watch and declared it Need to Stop Looking at my Watch Day... I've been watching my second-hand watch for some time now... and can tell you that this first-hand knowledge of the second-hand can really be a waste-of-time... so I'm going online to book my watch on a flight so I can watch it fly and so I can start having fun again..."

He put the book away, and then lit a Hav-A-Tampa sweet cigar. "To be forgotten by readers, colleagues and critics who once praised you is a hell of a lot like wearing a wet wool blanket in the middle of an August heat wave with lots of holes in the damn thing. Ah, but I digress..."

"You're a writer?"

"Well, I fell on hard times and developed an addiction to crack cocaine, had to declare bankruptcy after attempting to finance a play I'd written and ended up living in the Salvation Army homeless shelter...Unfortunately, I've been unable to maintain my sobriety and the shelter requires regular drug tests... but I'm keeping hope alive, as they say, as well as keeping my options open, whatever options happen to be open to me, that is... ah, but don't despair, I see that look on your face, a combination of pity and horror, but I'm still very much of a glass half-filled kind of guy... I used to be the other kind, you know, the half-empty guy, but it really wasn't working for me... I read that book, 'The Power of Positive Thinking' and also the one by Norman Cousins, what the hell's the name of it...? Anyway, Cousins' also believed in the power of a positive attitude...and laughter... he'd watch Marx Brothers movies...he survived years beyond what his doctors predicted... fascinating story..."

"'The Anatomy of an Illness'."

"What's that?"

"The name of Norman Cousins' book."

"Yes, of course, thank you... how could I forget that? Wonderful book... So it's totally a mind-over-matter thing... it's like my friend at the Chinese restaurant down the street... every day he gives me a fortune cookie because he believes in me, he really wants me to bounce back..." He reached into his pocket, pulled out the latest fortune and read it. "'Don't underestimate yourself. Your social skills are needed by others at this time.' How perfect is that for a guy like me...? I'm telling ya, I'm about to turn over a new leaf, I can feel it."

"That's great."

"It's all in here," he said, tapping the cover of the notebook. "Just need to find somebody willing to take a chance on me."

"Any prospects?"

The tramp smiled, but I could tell it was really a frown pretending to be a smile. "The world is full of prospects... as my friend at the Chinese restaurant always says, 'A book tightly shut is but a block of paper'..." Then, opening the notebook, he said, "'But open it up and it is like a garden'... Just needs a little more cultivation, you know, and a little weed control... but it's all in here...just need to find somebody willing to take a chance on me..."

"Well, I wish you luck, sir," I said.

"You're very kind, thank you... you err...wouldn't happen to be a patron of the arts, by any chance, would you...? I could really use your support..." He drew a nearly empty fifth of whiskey from beneath his coat. "A writer's gotta have a little inspiration, you know..."

I grabbed a few bucks from my pocket and gave it to him.

"Son, I really do appreciate this... listen, do me a favor..." He removed a small pencil from inside the spiral rings of the notebook. "Lemme get your name and address... soon as I get my advance, I'm gonna pay you back..."

"That's not necessary," I said.

"Please," said the tramp.

"Consider it a grant."

The tramp slipped the bills into his pant's pocket and smiled. I could tell he meant it this time. "Bless you, my son" he said, and he walked away singing "Beautiful Dreamer".

she suffers well

She was svelte and blond and from
Louisville, Kentucky,
6'3" in heels.

Within the first 3 minutes of
meeting me, she announced drily
that Paxil and Prozac couldn't fix
her personality and she was now
putting the responsibility
of fixing it squarely on my shoulders.

Over a plate of beans and onions
she confessed to having a
pool-hall education.

"And am I the only one who feels
uncomfortable watching old men
playing with babies?" she said.
"The only one who can't look a
stroke victim in the eye when
they're talking?
Or figure out what to say to
somebody in a wheel chair?
And why do I always get
chest pains whenever I read
from the New Testament?"

I asked her if she had ever considered
becoming an observational comic.

She shook her head and said,
"I'm only funny when I'm menstruating."

And while explaining to her how I received
teeth marks on the thumb of my left hand,
she interrupted me and said,
"I once dated a guy into coprophilia and urolagnia...

Lemme tell you, man, there is nothing
erogenous about feces and urine,
I don't care how horny I am, OK?"

During the cab ride home,
as she lit her twentieth clove cigarette
of the night, she said,
"We're so doggone quick to believe
celebrities who admit to entertainment
reporters how they've been battling
with depression all their lives and so quick
to doubt our own family members who
suffer from the same affliction…"

We made plans to go moonlight bowling
the following weekend, but when I called
her a couple days later her roommate
told me she had quit her job and moved
to Las Vegas to learn to become a croupier.

I hung up, stared at those teeth marks
on the thumb of my left hand and decided
that the story of how I received them
probably deserved to be interrupted.

a spiritual sort

It was one of those parties where the guests were all under-dressed, smoking from Hookahs, drinking either Cosmopolitans or Long Island Iced Teas.

Very few jokes were being told, mostly people were looking at each other, sighing through their smoke rings, avoiding eye contact. When an anecdote was disclosed, it usually ended with the protagonist becoming an alcoholic, going bankrupt, suiciding, or faking their own death and moving to Bali.

The hostess, a thin, droopy-eyed spiritual sort, who was constantly complaining of a "cloudy stomach" (something in her G.I. tract), approached me with a smile and a glass of wine. "This is astonishingly good... I bought it at the 99 cent store... you won't believe how masterfully blended and smooth and flavorful it is..."

I tasted it. It wasn't bad. Sort of reminded me the wine my father used to make.

"In a blind taste test," the hostess said. "It won first prize among a group of retired wine makers and grape growers in Sonoma County."

Knowing nothing about wine, I just said, "Hmm, interesting..."

"So," she said. "How do you like the renovations to our house? My mother says the early American antiques and collection of folk art just doesn't go with the marble floors, the 18th century paneling and the bronze balustrades, but you know what? I like it."

And then this comment wafted through the air:

"It's funny when new money tries to look like old money, but it's sad when new money has no taste."

I absorbed the decor and gave it a subtle nod of approval. "I've never seen anything quite like it," I said.

The hostess smiled and waved to somebody across the room. "...Well, you know, everyone has a different idea about what good taste is. I'm not a purist, what can I tell you?... Would you excuse me? I need to speak to my nutritionist... try the onion Bhajias, they're wonderful..."

Before I could reach the hors'deserve table, I was accosted by the "Baby Rap" ringtone from my wireless. Embarrassed, I sneaked into the bathroom and sat down on the avocado green custom-built pull chain toilet.

"Yeah," I said.

"So did you make up your mind yet?"

It was April, a girl who'd recently become more than just a booty call to me, according to her.

Over the last few months, she'd been pressuring me into giving something of a commitment to her, but when I told her I was too tired to get into a relationship, she took out her iPhone, searched for the calendar and said, "I'm giving you until April 1st to make up your mind...if you haven't made up your mind by April 1st, then," she shrugged. "Oh well..."

"Oh well?" I said.

"That's correct..."

"What is that supposed to mean?"

She shrugged again and walked away.

I looked at my watch. It was April 1st.

"Nice day, isn't it?" April said.

"Yeah, it's April Fools Day, isn't it?" I said.

"All day..."

"Yaaa... been fooled by anybody today?"

"I don't know," April said. "It's still early..."

"Riight…"

There was a pause.

It was so pregnant it was about to give birth to quintuplets.

"Where are you?" April said.

"I'm at a party…"

"Oh really? Whose?"

"Some coworkers…"

"Ohh…"

Pause.

There was a knock on the door.

"Occupied!" I said.

"Occupied?" April said.

"I'm in the bathroom…"

"Lovely…"

I glanced at the original French double ended cast iron roll top bath with ball and claw feet and the antique gold finish flush pipe set and thought, *why?*

"*Hello!*" April said.

"I'm here."

She started humming the theme from Jeopardy.

She was probably thinking this was the point in the story where I was supposed to discover my maturity and undergo some kind of transformation in which I gain new knowledge about myself, resulting in me becoming more moral and self-responsible than before.

But apparently my time had run out.

"Ooooh, sorry," April said, feigning disappointment. "Nice try, though. Thanks for playing," and she hung up.

I walked outside, onto the recently stained deck where a group of elderly men were involved in a heated discussion about whether or not Karl Marx was a false prophet. The man with the hairless, boney legs shook his fist in the air and shouted, "The man was so personally charming, that he..." But he didn't get to finish his posit because he began hacking from not taking in enough oxygen in between sentences. His main antagonist, an 80 year old former beatnik, in an Abercrombie & Fitch sweatshirt and New York Yankees hat, laughed at the hacking man, slapped him on the back, said, "Statistics strike again!"

That's when I got in my car and drove away.

her journey parallels her character's journey

Woman in Peril said, "How you gonna jump
into a relationship four months after you
separated from your wife?

How you gonna do that?

Then have the nerve to tell your soon-to-be ex-wife
you're in love with a girl nearly half your age?

How does that work?

He doesn't love her.

He's infatuated with her.

Has nothing to do with love.

He's infatuated with the idea of havin'
a little young thang on his arm.

He says, 'You can't tell me I'm not in love'

Yeah? You wanna bet? You're not in love.
Lust is not love. Love is love. Infatuation is not love, okay?

He says, 'Why can't you just accept it?'

Because, motherfucker, you're still a married man.
Separated or not, we're still married.

He doesn't get that.

Bottom line, he's committing adultery.

In God's eyes, it's adultery.

But, see, he's living in this strange sorta moral universe
where it's okay for him to screw around like that.

In his eyes, there's nothing wrong about what he's doing.

Because he's rationalizing.

"Me and my wife are separated, therefore, it's okay.
'Sides, I'm in love with this chick."

It's not love.

But I'm not worried about it 'cuz God'll have the
final say and make things right.

God will determine his destiny for him, so,
I'm not worried about it.

He can do what he wants.

Cuz judgment day will solve everything for his ass."

the dust of everyday life

Picasso was talking to a group of elementary school kids.

He approached the blackboard and scribbled something on it.

None of the children could figure out what it was.

It looked like an elephant with a ram's horn attached to its trunk.

One of the tikes whispered loud enough for Picasso to overhear, "That elephant has a penis where its trunk is supposed to be!"

Picasso twisted around and screamed, "Believe in the world of the unseen...for only then will you prepared to confront the tragedy of your own reality..."

The teacher, a prim, sexy little thing with a mole in the center of her chin, forced a smile and a small chuckle. "I think what Mr. Picasso is trying to say, boys and girls, is that, within every cloud there is a silver lining..."

Picasso's face contorted. His eyes bugged-out like somebody with a thyroid condition. The veins in his neck looked like blue worms squirming beneath his skin and he was frothing at the mouth. "You bitch! You ignorant, pathetic, little bitch!" He was now jumping up and down like a really pissed-off chimpanzee. "That is not what I meant at all! You have totally misrepresented everything I stand for! How you can stand in front of these children and present yourself as a teacher, is totally amazing!" He pointed wildly at the blackboard. "Tell me! Tell me what you see!"

The teacher fidgeted nervously. "Well," she said. "I-I-I-I...I see a-a-a rather...large...object, which...to me, appears to be a uhh...microbe, of sorts, perhaps...or some sort of...tissue or organism, or-or- division of cells? Perhaps in the final stages of either meiosis or mitosis...?"

She braced herself for another round of Picasso's wrath, but all she heard was the whirring, wobbling sound of a ceiling fan in need of repair.

Picasso stared strangely at the frightened educator. Something within him seemed to soften. And then finally, he spoke. "You really think so?" he said.

The teacher nodded cautiously. "Mmm hmm," she said.

Picasso turned to face his drawing again and studied it carefully. "Hmm, meiosis, mitosis…" He scratched the stubble on his chin with three of his fingers. "I've been drawing so many wrestlers lately, that I…" He trailed off, then turned his head back to face the teacher, whose eyes were busy avoiding him. "Look at me," he said.

She looked at his Adam's apple.

"Look into my eyes," he said.

Oh, God, they feel like lead right now, she thought. But somehow she managed to lift her eyes and rest them on what looked to her like two tiny lumps of bituminous coal inside the face of a deranged snowman.

"What is your name?" Picasso said.

"Nancy," she said.

"I want to draw you…I want to paint you…"

"I'm flattered, Mr. Picasso," she said. Then, with surprising courage, she added, "But I've seen what you've done to the faces of other women you've painted…"

"What I have done to them? What about what they have done to mine?"

Picasso paused and lit another cigarette. He began to sweat as he looked out into the befuddled faces of the children. He seemed to be asking them for something…Forgiveness? Their understanding? "You would all like me to draw a picture of your teacher, no?"

One of the girls in the back row raised her hand. "Is she gonna look like that?" she said, pointing to the drawing on the blackboard.

The children laughed.

Picasso smiled and looked at his drawing one more time. "I cannot promise she will look that good, but we will see…"

looking black upon me

She smokes cigarettes while
doing deep-breathing exercises.

Drinks coffee in order to
reach her target heart rate.

Has a way of whispering without
sounding like a conspirator.

Is the only one I know that
doesn't look like a fraud whenever
she's walking in the rain.

She once told me,
"There are two things you should never,
under any circumstances do,
while in the company of a woman:
make eye contact with her after
she's stuffed her mouth full of food
or look directly at her when she's
wearing sunglasses."

She and I tried to make a go of it
back in 90's, but she said she didn't
like "funny, sulky men."

Shortly after we separated,
I received a postcard from her
from San Francisco.

She was dating a man who was said to be
on "intimate terms" with her "G-Spot."

Her "God-Spot."

I never knew such a spot even existed.
I guess that's why she tried so hard to convert me.

her own private rapture

She'd be sitting alone,
drinking a glass of red wine in
a sparsely-populated bar
somewhere uptown,
staring into the strained and obvious light.

Inevitably,
some guy with beer nuts and
Budweiser on his breath
would accost her with some line like,
"Let's be laughing together next year," and
flash her a smile that usually reminded
her of those photographs her dentist
would show her, depicting the
beginnings of periodontal disease.

"Thanks," she'd say, "but it's not the right time
 in my life to be lowering my standards."

Sometimes the guy would laugh.

Sometimes not.

Usually not.

Which was fine with her.

What did she care if she pissed some guy off?

It was her life's work, in some ways.

After sitting and drinking for several hours,
she'd gather her stuff, and walk to a coffee shop or
an all-night movie theater.

Sometimes she'd go home and get her pocket-size Bible,
bring it with her and during especially boring moments,

turn to the Psalms or the Book of Daniel, Chapter 6,
which opens with the tribulation days,
when the anti-Christ comes on the scene riding a red horse,
and ask the nearest stranger,
"Have you had your own private rapture yet?"

Most people would squint hard,
shake their aching heads, and mutter something
over their breath like, "what a tormented soul."

She'd smirk at them,
sometimes show a toothy little grin, and close the Bible,
walk to the nearest payphone, and dial her latest lover;
usually a guy without disposable
income, often on disability from some accident on the job
or while serving their country.

"Yo," they'd say.

"What's goin' on?" she'd say.

"Shiiit..."

"Any news?"

"Bout what?

"I dunno – just lookin' for a little good news."

"Good luck," they'd say.

"You drunk?"

"Nope..."

"Sounds like it."

"Little wine's good for the heart."

"A little."

Usually a long pause here, followed by a silence known only to lonely women and fallen idols.

"I'll be home in a few minutes," she'd say.

"Take your time."

"Why?"

"Just kiddin'."

"Did you feed Roscoe?"

"Sure did."

"Half a can of Alpo, half a scoop of the dried food?"

"Yup."

Small pause here.

"I'll talk to you later."

"Adios."

She'd hang up, go back to the
sparsely-populated bar
somewhere uptown,
waiting for the next
guy with Budweiser and
beer nuts on his breath
to buy her a drink and say,
"Doesn't the rain make you blue?"

barfly tendencies

"Ever read a guy named Bukowski?" he said, stroking the scar on his thumb.

"Charles Bukowski?" I said.

He nodded.

"Some."

He smiled. Smirked, really. "He knew something," he said. Then looking away, he muttered something under his breath.

"What's that?"

Now his eyes were closed. "He knew about the logical progression of human beings."

"Hmm?"

"We progress from wearing our faces frontwards, to eventually..." He paused slightly. "Wearing them backwards." He shrugged. "The logical progression of human beings."

My instinct was to nod, but I figured it would only encourage him, so I stifled the impulse by thinking about a girl I used to know in Palo Alto, a certified financial planner, who kept trying to convert me to Scientology.

"Yep. Bukowski knew a thing or two," he said.

His nods were hypnotic. Infectious. Pretty soon I found myself nodding to the rhythm of his nod.

"Ever think you're misunderstood?" he said.

I had to think about that for a minute. "No, not really..."

"Hunh," he said, and ordered another vodka martini. "Life's such an aberration. When I was about twenty, twenty-five, I used to go around tellin' everybody I was misunderstood...didn't matter who it was...family, friends, strangers, Jehovah Witnesses...'course everybody's narcissistic and living a little too much in their heads at that age, but I was a fucking asshole about it...I'd monopolize every conversation...I'd make damn sure you were aware of what a complex guy I was, even though, you know, I was just some fucking asshole spoiled bitch with chips ahoys on my shoulder who didn't know the difference between pissing and fucking. It was all the same to me. Still is, to a point...but I've - hate this word - evolved - hate that word...I'm too old to have evolved...or should I say too insensitive..." He smirked. "But the shit of it all is, I got all kindsa pussy back then...and now?" He had a maniacal little smile. "Hardly get any at all...how does that work? Chrissakes, I haven't lost all my looks yet. Still gotta little sex appeal buried somewhere beneath this disheveled exterior...most a my hair's gone, alright, so, you know, a few wrinkles, but Jesus Christ, doth hair and a smooth face a man make?" His voice was becoming hoarse. He had to clear his throat several times. He reached into his coat pocket, pulled out a pack of Camel studs, and lit one. "Are you in love?" he said.

I shook my head.

"Have you ever been in love?"

I nodded.

"Have you ever run from love?"

I nodded.

He snickered. "I do the run-from-love in like two point five seconds... nobody can beat my time." He rubbed his eyes with the heals of his hands. "I get accused all the time of being too melancholy and not ambitious enough...hellava combination, boy...one without the other's difficult enough, but you put 'em both together? Forget about it...it's a harsh reality, boy, but a reality you gotta reconcile yourself to or else risk a lifetime of..." He stopped himself. "Never attempt to perpetrate on five vodka martinis, it's a no-win situation." He rubbed his neck and winced. "Funny, how we keep going, though...and going and going and going..."

He paused a moment to see if I still had a pulse. "You're not saying anything…you okay?"

"I'm fine."

"Don't talk much, do ya?"

I shook my head.

He shrugged. "That's cool…talking's overrated, anyway…problem with people is they got too many opinions…not enough sitting around quietly meditating, watching their breath…so many contradictions, so little equilibrium…that's man right there in a nutshell for ya."

That's when the bartender approached him. "Call for ya."

"Who is it?"

"Some broad."

"Scuse me, kid," he said, getting up from his stool. "The triangle awaits." He limped toward a side door that said "Private" and disappeared behind it.

I signaled the bartender for the tab.

a mother's secret hope

I was dancing with my mother at my wedding.

She was a little drunk and rattling on and on.

"When I met your father he had his feet up on a desk in his dorm room. He'd just started growing a mustache and it looked god-awful. Sort of wispy. I knew he hadn't, didn't have much of a future, work-wise. Not that taking over his father's dry cleaning business meant he didn't have a future. It wasn't my future, I can tell you that. I shouldn't be admitting this to you. After all these years…darling, this is your day. And it's been such a lovely day. Rachel is so…she truly…has wonderful teeth... her bone structure is just... has she had her teeth capped?"

"No, Mom."

"You want to know if I regret marrying your father. He's a good father. He drinks too much, but so do I. You resent the fact that we don't have any money, don't you?"

"What?"

"Your father just never had any get-up-and-go. He was always so preoccupied with his model airplanes. How does a man spend half his life building model airplanes? He's been trying to sell them on eBay. Nobody wants them. It's breaking his heart."

"Mom. . ."

"Mm, you came out of me like a bat out of hell. What a funny little thing you were. The doctor said you looked like Winston Churchill. God, and here you are twenty-six years later. . . and you're leaving me."

"I'm not leaving you."

"I had so many aspirations and expectations of what our family was going to become. Isn't it funny how life shapes us? We truly have no control over our own lives. The gods truly have us on strings."

"Mom, can we just dance?"

"Of course we can. I was quite a good dancer when I was younger. And I had a good voice, too. Then your father got me smoking."

She laid her head on my shoulder and fell asleep.

We just stood there in the middle of the dance floor.

My father approached us.

"What did she, pass out?" he said.

"Looks like it."

"Jesus H. Christ. Lemme have her," he said, picking her up in his arms and carrying her off somewhere.

I sat down. Rachel joined me.

"What happened?"

"She just had a little too much to drink."

"Did you tell her you're not going to take over your father's business?"

"Not yet."

"When are you going to tell them?"

I took a sip of champagne. "I'll let you know."

Outside, my mother was just coming to as my father was setting her on the passenger seat of his Impala. "What's going on...are we..."

"We're just gonna sit out here for a minute," said my father, shutting the door, and getting in on the other side.

"Oh, God," my mother said, taking her sunglasses out of her purse and putting them on. "Did I...Please tell me I didn't pass out."

"Alright, I won't tell you," my father said.

My mother groaned, obviously embarrassed.

They were quiet for several minutes, and then she spoke.

"They're going to move away, Marty, you know that."

My father just nodded and went into another one of his secret depressions.

By the time I had finally gotten around to telling him I wouldn't be inheriting the family legacy, my father announced to us that he was retiring from the dry cleaning business in order to devote more time to his model airplanes.

a construct, a fallacy, a lie

Do you believe life is eternal?
Do you believe Mother Goose went
through menopause?
Do you realize how expensive
lobsters are?
Do you fathom a man
equipped
with a plastic heart
who may begin to live longer
or who may turn into a clone
as he sits home watching
"The Price is Right"
and "Family Feud"
or reruns of "Barnaby Jones?"
Wasn't he too old to be a cop?
He had white hair,
he must have been ninety.
'Course he had Betty
and Betty was nice.
But he had to be a hundred
if not two hundred
at least.
And he drove a Ford, I imagine
'cause all them cops do,
'cause America is the land of
Jesus and Ronald Reagan
and Stove Top Stuffing
instead of potatoes
'cause potatoes are
carbohydrates
and we all know what happens
to people when they eat
carbohydrates
like potatoes.
Only life was much nicer
when John Boy wrote in his
open window

about the lovely happenings
around him.
Did he ever get a rock thrown
at him
all those years
writing in an open window late
at night,
I wonder?
Did an apple ever careen off his head
or a stalk of corn
or pig shit from the barn?
Did he ever yell out the
window?
Did he ever say,
"You damn beauty mark you!"
Did he ever get mad at Olivia
and call her a bitch?
Or was life on Walton's Mountain just
like living in a tee pee
in Minnesota?
Eating wild rice,
vinegar,
and fruit juice.
Passing joints
and singing "Louie, Louie,"
even though we never knew the
words,
just sang them and
laughed.
It had something to do with
ladies feeling uncomfortable, didn't it?
Or was it about Margaret Truman's
agonizing autobiography
"How Come Harry Wore Holes in His Socks?"
Or did Henry Kissinger figure in?
It's doubtful.
Although, the accent fits,
but not like a glove.
Perhaps like a garbage bag
or can.
Or maybe we assume

the ridiculous
is just a matter of
ejaculating the awkward parts
and rejuvenating the
Soul
as we know it
to be
or not to be.
But I have the answer,
though the question was
ambiguous,
even though he wrote like a
madman.
Or was it really Marlowe
behind Julius Caesar
and Hamlet,
that fine young Dutch lad
with a penchant for suicide
since his mama called
him and told him she
never loved him,
just raised him 'cause he was cute
and deductible.
And as he stood
visa vi
with me
I said "Good-day"
and he crushed the skull
because it smelled funny.

often lost and forgotten

Ralph Ellison
wrote about
the invisible
man.

But guys like
me are
invisible, too.

Our
life's pace and
lack of urgency
make us almost
impossible to find.

We begin disappearing
early in life,
usually after our first
kiss.

And from that point on
we seem to vanish
in front of
all who
come within
eyeshot of us.

his shivering life

He thought back. To an earlier time. But the memory was fragmented. In pieces. Colliding with other memories. Just out of reach. Accessible to him only during rapid eye movement. In a room. No. In the womb. During a full moon. In June. Yes. That was the memory. In the womb. He recalled. Something. Somebody. Shouting. Then hushed whispers. Being yelled at. Then whispered to. How lonely. Rapid breathing. Heart beating. Sweats. Panic. Gasp of breath. Alone. Shouts and whispers. Then silence. The sound of a clock? Or the beating of a heart? A song? Voices in discord? No harmony. No melody, either. And very little rhythm. But sounds nonetheless. Guttural sounds. Guzzling sounds. Guy sounds. It was Good Friday, that day, even though my birth certificate says Easter Sunday. The rabbi had to drive in from Teaneck to perform the bris. He had a bad back. Garlic breath. Eyes kept blinking because he'd just been fitted with contact lenses. Said he didn't think they were ground right. Everyone said he looked like he was crying when he snipped off my foreskin. I for damn sure was. That much I remember. Nerves for days down there. And Rabbi Watery Eyes deadens the sensation for me forever. The family celebrates. Hard salami served on rye bread. Chopped chicken liver. Herring. Lox. Bagels. Bialys. Chala. Cream cheese. Kosher dills. Manischewitz wine. Schnapps. Hear all about it! Secular Jew born on Good Friday (or Easter Sunday), take your pick, who wants to argue?

a matter of mathematics and common sense

You left the party early.
Again.
Kept whispering in my ear,
"I have this social anxiety disorder.
I'm very uncomfortable. I'm sorry, I can't do this."

You were wearing clothes that had the
morning headlines written all over them and
I was anxious to do a readability index on you; but
you disappeared before I could even recall the
formula to measure it.

I figured I couldn't do anything for you, anyway,
but thought maybe I could have at least...

But probably not.

When I got home, I called you.
Got your voice mail.
You were probably hiding under the sheets.
Sweating.
Crying.
Petitioning somebody.
Maybe the Lord.
Maybe just your shrink.

Who knows?

You always held very secular beliefs.

Didn't laugh much in those days.
Hardly cracked a smile.
Slept twelve, thirteen hours a day.
Ate next to nothing.
Whenever you did have contact

with the world it was always from
a comfortable distance.

You were always reluctant to talk
about yourself.
Your past.
Your future.
Didn't even talk about your job
as a dispatcher for a cable TV company.

At night, you sat in front of the TV under
a blanket, even in July and August.

Kept your thermostat at 60 year round.

"One way or another I get what I need,"
you told me the day before your birthday.

You were turning thirty.
I came over.
Gave you a present.
A papier-mache elephant.
You about cried, but laughed instead.

Fortunately, my feelings weren't hurt.

But then again I was a lot better at
compartmentalizing my feelings in those days.

just part of this ether

I was one of those wayward guys who drank bourbon and read pulp fiction and smoked Chesterfield cigarettes.

I'd walk into a bar and begin railing against the government, my employer, my family, the last woman who'd rejected me.

Sometimes I'd get so drunk the bartender would have to call the police and they'd throw me in the drunk tank and I'd wake up the next morning wondering how the hell I'd got there.

I'd go home, shower and shave, get dressed, go into work late.

My supervisor would call me into his office.

"What's up?" he'd say.

"I'm late, I know," I'd say. "I'm sorry." Then I'd sort of shrug like that answered everything and say something really profound like "Life…"

My supervisor would watch me carefully, try to read my subtext. "Life, what?"

I wouldn't give it much thought beyond that. Figured it was enough of an explanation. But I knew I'd have to say something else because I was sitting in front of my supervisor who could fire me without much cause because I lived in a right-to-work state.

"Well, sir," I'd begin, and then I'd desperately search for something else to say. But what was there to say?

At that point I'd usually come clean.

Or more accurately, slightly soiled.

"I was up all night…couldn't sleep…just thinkin' about a lot of things… finally fell back to sleep about five, five thirty…thought I'd set the alarm, but I guess I hadn't…oldest excuse in the book, I know…but it's true…it won't happen again…"

"Are you okay? You seem a bit distracted."

"I'm fine, sir. Have a lot on my mind. But as I said, that's no excuse…"

"You know we have an employee assistance program…"

"Yes, sir, I know; I appreciate that. I'm fine. Just need a good night's rest."

I'd go back to my cubicle, think about quitting again.

Then I'd put my headset on and get that first call of the day.

"Emergency Crisis Hotline," I'd say.

"I'm feeling very depressed," the caller would say.

I'd push the mute button on my phone console, take a deep breath, recall when I existed in the world, before everything was blue and make one last private plea for my day to end in at least one small victory.

tryin' to git it back in my soul

She came at me with those baby blue infant eyes and said, how you feeling baby, and I just sort of shrugged and mumbled something and she said what'd you say and I shook my head and tried to play it off, whatever it was I was trying to play off. She said she was beginning to get concerned, I said concerned about what, she said concerned with the state of my mind, I said life is a state of mind, she said wha'cha mean, I said I'm not really sure but all I know is I'm waiting like Godot and it's scary as hell being so alone like this with my feelings.

Then, shining a light deep within me, she showed me those parts of me I tried to keep hidden. I was scared. She didn't care. She just kept shining that light in me. Want you to feel it, she said. You gotta get it out. It's deep. Down there deep. You gotta get it out or else you're gonna be stuck. And then where you gonna be? It's not healthy. It's suffocating you. Sitting home all day. Moaning. Crying. Can't do that. Eatin' you up. It's gotta stop. You gotta come to terms with it.

She shined that light so deep in me I was feeling things I hadn't felt in twenty thirty forty tears, felt like something was about to climb out of me. All those crazy feelings I'd kept hidden from the general public. Churning away, blending together. It was rough.

Feel the pain, she said. Feel it like a knife cutting into your heart. Feel it like that.

But I've run into a snag, I told her. I can't find the words to express all that pain inside of me. I don't know how to interpret the pain. I need a translator. But who's gonna be able to translate all that mess? No one but me. But I don't know what it all means. I don't know what happened to me. I don't know why I keep stopping and starting, being all mute, disengaged, disinterested, disconnected, distant. In disbelief. Disarray. Want to disappear. Feel so much disapproval.

That's when the trumpet solo began.

She said listen to Lee Morgan. He can help you articulate all that pain you're feeling. Just listen to him play the trumpet. He's feeling what you're feeling right now. He's lost something. He's trying to forget something. Remember something. Not sure where he's going, but he's following a path. Hear that? He's remembering something. Someone he knows lives somewhere along that path. Hear the way he's fingering those valves? You feel it honey? You see it? Touch it, taste it. It's your pain. Lying there.

I'm trying to see it, I said. I can't quite see it yet. It's somewhere in there. It's a little blurry. I can kind of feel it but I can't see it. Not yet. I want to say it's blue, though. It's like the blue coming from Lee Morgan's trumpet.

Yes baby that's what I'm talking about. The blues. The beautiful blues.

It's there, I said. It's there. I felt those blues years ago. I remember now. I used to be afraid of the blues. When I was younger. They'd come find me, I'd hide. But I'm still hiding. I'm gonna be forty six, I'm still hiding.

I know you are baby. Hiding from the light. Hiding from the blues. But the blues gonna find you one way or another and you're gonna have to welcome the blues into your life. No matter how rude it is. No matter what kinds of demands it makes on you. You're gonna have to look the blues in the eye and make some kind of sense of it.

Yeah, I said, I will.

That's it baby that's it. Feel it. Where's the pain coming from? Who was the cause of it? Who you gonna blame it on this time? You gotta conquer it baby. Make it your slave.

I took a deep breath. I tried to think of something. Remember something. Tried to hum that Lee Morgan trumpet solo. It was singing to me. I could feel Lee Morgan speaking to me. I could feel his pain. Why couldn't I feel mine? I was beginning to breath a little deeper. Could feel the muscles in my neck and back tightening up. I didn't really want to say anything that might incriminate me. I was still uncertain of what all those feelings meant. They were still buried very deep within me. And then I felt my heart flutter. Slight pain in my wrist. Numbness. My foot was falling asleep.

Where you going in your head baby, she said. Where you going now?

I don't know. I'm thinking about a time when someone mistreated me. Or maybe I mistreated them. My memory of it is still a little hazy. Can't even remember if somebody did something to me or if I did something to them. Or did something to myself.

Now you're beginning to get to the root of something baby, she said.

The root, I said. The root. I paused. Tried to recall the meaning of the word. Root. Figure out its context. Her context. Chest pain. Back muscles stiff. Head cool. Mouth dry. Left wrist numb. Deep breath. It's never easy, I said. Never easy bein' me.

Aw now you're just being self pitying, she said. No need for that now. Listen to Pharaoh Sanders. There's a master plan somewhere inside of you. You just gotta find it.

Yeah, I said, without really knowing what she said or meant. I swallowed. Scratched my chest. Why was it so hard for me to get to the root of my pain? Why did I keep sidestepping it? Just for Comfort's sake? I swallowed again. Lit a cigarette. Poured a bourbon. Scratched my chest again. She was still there, watching me. I was feeling very self-conscious. I didn't want her to be watching me. I felt like I was on display. A Pain Artist. Sitting there. But it was unfair because it seemed like she was more aware of my pain than I was. She was just sitting there waiting for me to discover my own pain while she knew what it was all along. I didn't like that. She was even smiling, daring me to figure out my pain, challenging me to dig deeper.

Yeah yeah yeah yeah yeah yeah yeah yeah yeah.
The Creator has a master plan.
Peace and happiness for every man.
The Creator makes but one demand
Happiness through all the land.

Listen to Pharaoh, she said.

Yes, I said, I want peace and happiness. I want to find peace and happiness. I'm not sure how to find it, though. It's like I'm punishing myself for something. I'm stopping myself from progressing. I'm punishing myself for... I stopped there. I didn't know what I was punishing myself for. I just didn't know what else to say.

You can't fall asleep now, she said. You'll lose the momentum. You'll lose all the good work you've done. You'll forget everything. You'll have to start from scratch again tomorrow.

I haven't done anything, I said. I haven't accomplished anything yet. All I've done is listen to you tell me I've got to dive deeper and listen to Pharaoh's sax and Lee Morgan's trumpet.

Because what you're feeling is in the music. You got to listen to the music. Then you'll be able to express your feelings.

Yeah, I said, and then the radio played Adam's Apple by Wayne Shorter and that made me think of the Garden of Eden. I smiled and laughed and she said what's so funny and I told her nothing, it was just a nervous reaction or something. Then the sadness I was feeling last week started coming back strong. It happened while I was driving into work. I just started thinking about where the hell the last ten years of my life had gone, man? Where'd they go? And why'm I still working for the same company doing the same job? That reality hit me real hard. The truth of that nearly broke me. And it was raining and I almost slammed into the car in front of me that was stopped at a red light. That's how engrossed I was in that sad feeling. I missed slamming into the rear end of that Cadillac by only a couple feet or so. And my heart started racing. And the rain kept coming down. And my windshield fogged up, so I turned on the defroster. All because of that sad feeling I was experiencing about working for the same company and doing the same job for ten years. That was a real eye opener for me.

Ah, she said, my poet. Dreamer. Lonely fellow. Boots too big, trousers baggy, shirt untucked, Kangol hat too small.

I poured another bourbon, became even more frightened.

It was going to be another long night.

there were no secrets kept that night

It's Christmas Eve. It's raining. None of the presents are wrapped. We're watching "Rudolph the Red-Nose Reindeer". Brittany cries when all of the other reindeer laugh and call Rudolph names. Raphael's roasting chestnuts. Chelsea's reading an article in Teen People about stigmata.

The phone rings.

Nobody answers it.

"I'm at home in almost any environment," Courtney says, after introducing herself as The Castrating Bitch.

That's when I bail on 'em.

Go upstairs to my bedroom. Kneel beside my bed unselfconsciously. Pray, for a change.

Knock knock, "You okay?" says an unrecognizable voice.

"Fine!" I say.

"We're playing Monopoly! Wanna play?"

I finally place the voice. It's Sunshine, the platinum blond transvestite.

"No thanks!" I say.

Platform shoes walk away.

The wind picks up.

I overhear the following snatch of dialogue in the hallway.

"I have a degree in biology from Vassar... Plants can reproduce sexually or asexually... See? Tol'ja I have a degree."

Outside my window, the carolers have hunkered down. They're in their rain coats and standing under golf umbrellas.

"Hark the herald angels sing…"

One of the carolers has forgotten the words. I open the window. Fortunately, I don't slip a disc. I start singing. Basically on key. Wet, but on key.

The carolers cringe.

Then knock knock. "We're going out!" says the chick with the Band-Aid on her chin.

A debacle of epic proportions, I think.

"No thanks!" I say without any guilt.

Galoshes walk away.

In the distance I hear you explaining Immaculate Conception to 7 year old Gabriel.

"Mary," you say. "Was conceived without sin. And Jesus was born to Virgin Mary through a miraculous act of God…"

Gabriel thinks about this for a minute. "Is that how I was born, too?" he asks.

"Uhm, not exactly," you say. "But you are a miracle."

Gabriel understands almost all of it except the part about being conceived without sin.

"My teacher said that Sin is a Mesopotamian moon god."

"Really," you say.

"Yep," Gabriel says, going back to his room to blow his horn.

That's when sleep takes hold of me.

And I dream, once again, of being a child in a manger.

.

final draft

I

With an eclipse in the sky,
a bottle of Remy by his side,
and a bowler on his head,
The Follower, inert and enervate,
pulled a paperback from his knap
sack entitled, "Smirking at the Unfinished
Novel in the Bottom Desk Drawer," and
read a passage from it:

"Peckinpaugh was an enigma. As a tragic hero, there was something
Shakespearean about him. There were also grounds to classify him as a
psychiatric case, bordering on insanity. Twenty years of anxiety,
temperament, and unhappiness had earned him his first heart attack at the
age of forty-two. He'd lived an unbelievably depressing, dirty, and drunk
life; his home, to all practical purposes, was a room at the YMCA..."

The Follower closed the book,
stroked his forehead.

He was taking a new medication that
made him sleepy.

II

Returning to his sparse, dim room,
The Follower poured himself a glass of scotch,
and then began to dictate his biomythography
into a portable MP3 recorder.

"'The Grinning Visage,' subtitled 'The Pathos of the Lie.'
Chapter one. Like most people, he was complicated..."

The Follower paused the recorder and waited for the next line.

Fifteen minutes later, he spoke into the microphone again.

"Like most people he was complicated.
He bled self-pity. No one could take a joke so personally..."

That's when it dawned on him that he was
writing about a truth
that would have killed most men.

He learned about this truth early in life.

There was always an obvious silence in the house,
the kind that cut gaping holes in him.

Nobody ever said good morning.

They just looked at each other and sighed.

Whenever words were exchanged,
they were usually uttered in harsh whispers.

Secrets were guarded and disclosed only
if they betrayed somebody's trust.

Lies were elaborate and endless and never agonized over,
and truth was something that was always referred to in
the past tense.

The Follower poured another scotch and, forgetting to turn on the record
button, spoke softly into the microphone.

"Weary, exhausted and fueled by my pretenses, I found rhythms and
myths. I wandered, then followed my faults to the ends of the needles
being jabbed into my veins. While on my way to waterfront motels, I
developed intense distrust of women. I was fascinated by them. At the
same time I felt I had no idea what was going on inside of me and to get
close to a woman was to risk entrapment, imprisonment and
claustrophobia. But now there I was. I was in America, God's country,
driving in an American Machine, taking deep breaths, then shallow
ones..."

And in a breeze, The Follower's consciousness was no more.

i put up some brave fronts in those days

I'd walk into a bar on Sunset Boulevard
and look for the nearest whore.

What else was there to do?
My self-esteem was lower than Kafka's.

I'd sit at a table in the corner,
order something that would get me drunk as my old man
and begin giving the eye to the whores;
I was in love with whores back then.
I had to have a different one every night
or else I'd get a headache.
Didn't matter what they looked like;
although I was partial to blacks and Asians,
especially Asians with pretty feet cause
I have a foot fetish and like to put my cock
between their silky toes and jerk off till
I bust a nut.

Ah but I digress…

I'd order a 7&7 and pretend I was somebody,
wink at the waitress,
try to get her number,
but she'd gimme the old brush-a-roo and
I'd go home with another one of my whores and
come hard all over her belly, lye in bed, have conversations like,

"Sounds like your life is really kinda sad and sketchy," she'd say.

"Only if you look too closely at it."

She wouldn't know what the hell to say to that,
but she'd really feel sorry for me,
kind of like the way you feel sorry for a dog
when you're eating a T-bone steak and he can't take his eyes off you.

Sometimes she'd tear up and I'd say,
"For a whore you're pretty emotional."

She'd slug me,
I'd pass out,
wake up a an hour later.

She'd still be there,
sitting on the edge of the bed,
staring at me,
sipping a French liqueur,
looking like a Chekhov heroine on heroin.

I'd feel my face with my fingers,
ask her if I had a black eye,
she'd shrug and say something like,
"It compliments your inner demons,"
and I'd grizzle.

I'd offer her a cigarette,
we'd sit there smoking and
focusing on the sensations
of our bodies
until the sun came up.

Then she'd crush her cigarette out
in the ash tray,
get dressed,
fix her hair,
touch up her makeup,
strike a pose.

"How do I look?" she'd say.

"Sexually ambivalent," I'd say.
"How do I look?"

She'd study my face,
a little too closely.
"Dank-faced and disheveled;
like you're self-conscious about sharing

too much of your personality
because you're afraid
others will judge or criticize you."

I'd nod but wouldn't say anything,
mostly because of my pride,
but also because I figured you
don't always have to say something
just because somebody makes a
dead-on observation of you;
sometimes you can just sit there quietly
and let them wonder why you're not
saying anything.

Eventually, she'd realize she'd have to keep it moving;
too many gaps and silences in our conversations,
not a compelling enough emotional arc for her to care enough
about our little tale to follow it through to the end.

She'd say "Au revoir, mes enfant,"
I'd nod slowly and watch her walk out the door.

I'd sit at my desk,
drink some whiskey,
listen to some Monk,
write some poems.

"Even sad sex is better than no sex at all," I'd think,
and sure enough, my headache would be gone.

she will love you more than any other guy

She was twenty-nine or thirty.

One of those women who'd get angry with you if you bought her a gift that had a chord attached to it.

Who treated a man like a fruit salad. "I like this but I don't like that…like this but not that…this, not that."

The day we met, she inspected my shoes.

"Hm, wing tips," she said. "You're all business."

"Well, they're just one of the pairs of shoes I own," I said.

"Have any Chuck Taylors?"

"No, I don't. Do I get points deducted for that?"

"No, but you get points deducted for asking me if you get points deducted for that."

"Sorry."

She looked at my watch. "Hmmm…"

"Hmmm?"

"I like your watch."

"It was a present from my grandfather."

"That's a fascinating story. Why is wearing a watch so important to you?"

"I just like the way it looks."

"Good answer; time, after all, is completely irrelevant," she said, sarcastically.

"'The laws of science do not distinguish between the past and the future'."

She stared at me for several seconds. "Do you quote often from Stephen Hawking?"

"You're familiar with Hawking?"

"I'm studying theoretical physics."

"Wow, what are the odds of that? No, actually, it's like the only quote of his I've ever committed to memory…and I don't even know why that one stuck with me."

She put her right forefinger to her lips and shushed me.

A few minutes later in my apartment, as I handed her a glass of cognac, I toasted to bigger and better days.

"Define bigger and better days," she said.

I thought about it for a minute. But I didn't know exactly how to answer her question. So I didn't. I took a sip of cognac instead, completely avoiding her eyes. But she was one of those gals who could see right through guys like me and so she pressed me further.

"Define bigger and better days," she said.

I waited twenty or thirty seconds before speaking.

"Independence," I said, barely able to contain my jitteriness.

"From what?" she said.

Why couldn't she just accept the first thing that came out of my mouth, I thought. Why did she have to be one of those skeptical chicks? I'd about had my fill of skeptical chicks. Weren't there any wide-eyed idealistic hassle-free women left in the world? Did they all have to be such raging feminists?

"Independence from fear," I said, hoping this bullshit would fly.

She suddenly smiled. It was a sincere smile, too; the kind of a smile that was completely involuntary and didn't have an agenda. "You're a very spiritual man, aren't you?" she said.

"I have my days," I said.

"You can think on your feet, too. I like that in a man."

"Well, I'm pretty good at thinking lying down, too," I said.

"Are you?"

"But I'm at my very best when I'm on my knees."

She laughed. I liked her laugh. It made me feel like I could climb Mt. Everest butt naked.

"When I first met you," she said. "I thought you were gay."

I cleared my throat. "Oh really?

"You were listening to 'Dreamgirls on your iPod."

"You could hear it?"

"Sort of threw me for a minute."

I shrugged. "What can I say, I was brought up on show tunes. My parents loved Broadway."

"But then I realized there's no way in hell this guy's gay."

I questioned her with my eyebrows.

"You have that look of oblivion I've only seen on straight men."

I nodded like I knew what she was talking about. But I didn't. Truth was, I was having difficulty reading between her subtle, squiggly little lines.

But that was okay.

Because she was a discreet and exclusive New York City escort, and like a bottle of 2002 D'Anbino Paso Robles Syrah, she went down smooth and slow.

in the now of the now

I'm standing on the corner, trying to score something that will help me see the gods.

My mobile rings and I look at the caller ID and see it's the Candy Man and I answer it.

"Where you at?" I say and he says, "Between here and there," and I cut through the park where all the kids are trying to con their babysitters into letting them stay a half hour longer, and cross a street that doesn't seem to go anywhere. People are driving up and down it, but they have this look on their faces like they'd rather be somewhere else.

I turn left on Timothy Leary Boulevard, then right on Ernest Hemingway Place, then left on Jack Kerouac Street, then continue straight on William S. Burroughs Lane, and end at Richard Brautigan Avenue.

By this time, I can smell the Candy Man; a combination of lemongrass, jasmine, eucalyptus and peppermint, and I've found if you stand next to him long enough, he usually has a hell of an influence on your limbic system.

I approach him.

He's sitting Indian style under a ficus tree, reading from an old textbook.

He invites me to sit down next to him and schools me to something he's just learned.

"Reading about Sophocles, man," he says. "You know what he said?"

"No, what did he say?"

"To never have been born may be the greatest boon of all... ain't that a trip?"

"Wow."

He repeats what he's just quoted and lets it hang out there in the breeze for a minute or two and when he thinks I've really absorbed what he's just told me, he says "That's deep," and then a few seconds later he repeats that, too.

After about an hour or so of imparting all that worldly knowledge and wisdom on me, the Candy Man pushes his hand deep into the pocket of his old overcoat, pulls out a vial of something he calls "Dionysian Goo," hands it to me and says, "Here's a miracle dipped in a dream, my friend. It should really take you to somewhere not of this world."

I thank him and scamper off into the woods where I lay down by a creek and focus on my spiritual alchemy.

Eventually I drift off to sleep and experience that recurring dream where I'm trying to run away from some people. A woman who's eyes don't lie standing at a living room window, nursing a glass of red wine saying, "If not for love, then why?" A gravely-serious man with self-delusion in his eyes who's craving connection but can't break through. A child filled with luminous details submerged in a remote forested lake whose eyes seem to contain worlds of pain, loneliness, and grief.

And then I wake up.

I'm being escorted by an ex-girlfriend from the county jail.

"They popped you for public drunkenness," she says. "You blew an impressive 0.175, roughly twice the legal limit. They arrested you at the scene, took you to the county jail, I posted your bond."

"Thanks," I say.

"Gettin' a little old for this kinda shit, aren't you?"

I mumble something incoherent, get in her car.

She drops me off at the men's shelter.

I lie down on my cot; listen to the guy on cot next to me mumbling, "Treachery, betrayal, and rivalry boiled over as my hunt continued for…"

And he's asleep.

I reach for my journal, the one my case worker told me to start keeping, and write, What am I hunting for? Maybe for a chance to see all this primal rage and self-pity change to exultation.

I close my journal, stash it under my pillow, lie on my back, and stare at the slow rotating ceiling fan right above my cot.

And then my mobile rings and I look at the caller ID and see it's the Candy Man but I don't answer it.

The guy on the cot next to me continues mumbling. "At some point I'll return home…"

That's about how I'm feeling right now, too, homes, I think.

And I doze off.

i think my life story needs a rewrite

I feel the tears behind the curtains of my eyes
waiting in the wings for their grand entrance,
waiting for their cue,
waiting for the actors on stage to deliver their lines,
waiting for the audience's reaction,
the critic's reviews,
hoping that the show won't close
after tonight's performance.

she likes music in the key of g-minor

She went to a therapist.

"Why are you here?" said the therapist.

"I don't know why I'm here."

"You don't know?"

"I'm not sure."

"Surely you must have had a reason."

"My family thought I should come.   They felt my behavior was in noncompliance."

"Noncompliance?"

"Yessir."

"I'm not understanding."

"After reading an abnormal psychology text book, it was determined by my mother and father that my personality significantly deviated from the average...and so they suggested I see a therapist."

"What sort of behaviors were you exhibiting for them to come to that conclusion?"

"I was just being myself."

"Do you believe that your personality significantly deviates from the average?"

"No, sir, I don't."

"Who's going to be paying for this therapy?"

"My parents."

"And are they aware of my fee?"

"My family has very deep pockets. They said money is no object."

"How did they find me?"

"The yellow pages. They liked the fact that you're Jewish. They said all the best shrinks are Jewish."

"But there are hundreds of Jewish therapists in the yellow pages."

"My mother liked the sound of your name. She said she chose it because she saw a documentary about some holocaust survivors and one of the survivors that was interviewed in the movie had your name and she felt it might bring me good luck."

"I see...well...I, personally feel there's no reason for you to be here. I mean, you know what your problems are. You already know this. You don't need me to tell you what your problems are."

"Yessir."

"But if you'd like to continue with the process, I'd be more than willing to take you on as a patient."

"Well, sir, if I may be frank with you..."

"By all means"

"I would prefer not to."

"I understand."

"'Cuz then I gotta get in the car and drive here and fight all that traffic and find a place to park and it's a hassle. It just takes too much time."

"May I ask how you spend your time?"

"Well, I'm currently studying the Kabbalah.   I consider myself very mystical. Are you familiar with the Kabbalah?"

"Yes, I am."

"Madonna's like all over it…it's like the big thing in Hollywood… anyway, I'm just really beginning to get into it, I mean, it's very complex, as you probably know, there's a lot to digest, and I'm a little overwhelmed at the moment, but, my boyfriend, he's like the Real Mystic of the two of us, I'm just like a Mystic in Training…he picks up on all kindsa things in the Kabbalah, it's almost spooky how aligned with the universe he is… we're both Catholic, but very open to other religions; for instance, we're going to Rosh Hashanah services this Friday…yeah, that's kinda neat… will you be going to services…?"

"Uhh, no. I observe it in my own way."

"Oh…does that mean you don't attend synagogue?"

"My house serves as my family's spiritual epicenter."

"Mm, that's an interesting way of putting it…I understand… religion's one of the three things you're not supposed to talk about in public… sex and politics are the others, right?   Oh well…didn't mean to make you uncomfortable…I was just curious…"

"That's okay."

"Don't worry, I won't ask you if you're against abortion." she said, giggling. "Can I ask you this, though?"

"Sure."

"If you had three wishes, what would they be?"

The therapist thought for a moment. "I've never really thought about it. What would you do if you had three wishes?"

"Well, number one, I'd like to write novels…I'd like to be able to sing… that's two…" She paused. "Oh and I'd like Jack to ask me to marry him."

"Jack is your boyfriend?"

"Yes…we've been going out for three years… he's forty-nine…I'm thirty-two…that's kind of an age spread… but not really…he acts like a kid most of the time anyway…most men do."

"And is he moving in the direction of asking you to marry him?"

"Not really. He's been married. Twice. He really has no desire. I'm not even sure he loves me all that much anymore."

"Why do you say that?"

"He told me."

"He told you he doesn't love you?"

"Not in so many words. I pick up things from his body language."

"What kinds of things?"

"He doesn't like to kiss me anymore…or touch me…or make love to me… or have dinner with me… or watch TV with me…only thing he likes to do with me is read the Kabbalah…but he doesn't even like discussing it with me…hmm, wow, that's the first time I said that out loud…it doesn't sound too good, does it…?…I didn't mean for any of this to come out, I'm so sorry, I should go…uhm, will you send us a bill, or…?"

"I won't charge you."

"It's no problem, my parents can afford it."

"Don't worry about it."

"You sure?"

The therapist nodded.

"Sir, can you afford not to charge us?"

"I'll be alright," he said with a smile.

"Well…I thank you for your kindness…thank you for listening…you must be a very good therapist…"

"Thank you."

"I think if I ever had to go to a therapist, I would go to you."

"My door's always open."

"Well, I hope you and your family have a wonderful…observance of whatever you observe in your spiritual epicenter…goodbye…"

"Goodbye."

She walked to the door, but before her hand could touch the door knob, she turned back toward the therapist and said, "How much time do I have left?"

The therapist looked at his watch. "About a half an hour"

She paused. "Do you mind if I stay until my half-hour's up?"

"Not at all"

She walked back to the chair and sat down. "I'm a very good gin player," she said. "Would you like to play?"

"If that's what you'd like to do."

She reached into her purse, pulled out a deck of cards, and for the first time that day, she smiled.

waspy aversion to introspection

Meanwhile, Dr. Feel Alright was examining my neurosis.

"I've been looking at a lot of internet porn, lately," I said.

"I thought you were weaning yourself from all that," Dr. Feel Alright said.

I shrugged.

"The more you immerse yourself in it, the harder it will be for you to become intimate with a woman... It's been three years since you've been in a relationship. It lasted how long?"

"A few months..."

"What happened again?"

"She was too clingy. She needed to be held all the time and constantly reassured of how much I loved her, which I didn't. She was... I don't know, I guess you'd call her co-dependent..."

"I'd call her insecure."

"That too..."

"And there's been no one since?"

I stared at the floor.

"Why is that?"

I thought for a moment. "I'm too set in my ways..."

"What does that mean?"

The questioned unnerved me. "It means I'm not looking for anybody to change me."

"Change you? Or challenge you?"

My eyebrows twitched.

"Seems to me," Dr. Feel Aright continued. "That what you're most concerned about is somebody coming into your life and forcing you to actually be with another human being."

"Don't follow you," I said.

"Well, you've kept yourself pretty isolated over the years. You don't trust other people's motives and don't like the politics of interacting with others. You've said this to me repeatedly. You don't like having to engage in the politics at work. Don't like the politics of dating. You don't even vote because you don't like politics. This, to me, is like blaming your fear of the dark on the boogeyman. The boogeyman didn't create the dark. We're not even sure the boogeyman exists. But it's easier to blame the boogeyman, just as it's easier for you to blame politics, as opposed to trying to figure out why people create so much anxiety in you."

I was getting bored. I wanted to know how much time I had left in my session, but I was afraid to look at my watch because I knew she would see it as a sign of deception and avoidance; so I focused my eyes instead on a portrait of her family hanging on the wall. Her husband resembled Fred MacMurray, only he had a beard and black horn-rimmed glasses that made his eyes look like raisins, and he appeared as if he'd just leaned over to his wife just before the picture was taken and whispered, "Okay, let's hurry up and take this damn thing so I can get back to the office."

The children were fourteen year old fraternal twins. Her son's eyes looked a lot like mine. Unfocused. Cloudy. Dilated. They were the eyes of a real stoner. And her daughter's jaws were tensed; I imagined her pitching a major psychotic rage over being forced to participate in such an insane family ritual. I could tell, even from that corny portrait how miserable those children were. They didn't even look like they belonged there. They looked like they were either adopted or kidnapped. But it was my therapist who had the most curious expression. It was as if she had just been given some devastating piece of news prior to the photographer snapping the picture, and was desperately trying to conceal her emotions. It was an expression she had probably acquired over a period of years of having to endure patients like me.

"So what are your thoughts?" Dr. Feel Alright said.

I paused. "I miss my childhood," I said.

"Well, I think it's entirely normal and healthy to revisit the past in your mind and appreciate where you've been and enjoy the prior scenery. But I think it should be a short visit. Not a day trip. A kind of a, drop in on your aunt on your way to see your grandmother kind of a trip. I believe the goal of us all, every day and always, is to try and live in the present moment. Thoreau said it best. 'Only that day dawns, which we are awake.' I think you live too much in the past. I think we each have our own sensibility about how much reminiscing is too much, but I believe the more you enjoy the moment, the more you will appreciate your new surroundings and the more eagerly you will strive to explore the wonderful new places right out your front door."

I digested that. "Interesting," I said.

The alarm on her watch sounded. "We'll pick up on this in our next session… in the meantime…" Dr. Feel Alright handed me a sheet of paper. "I've got a homework assignment for you. Would like you to answer these questions and be prepared to discuss them next week."

I read the questions:

Who are you?
What do you want?
What was your father like?
Do you believe in God?
Who do you love?

"Questions?" Dr. Feel Alright said.

I shook my head.

"Getting a lot of non-verbals from you today."

I fidgeted in my chair a bit. "I'm fine."

She watched me closely. "See you next week?"

I waited before answering her. "That's fine," I said, feeling my thyroid cartilage jumping all over the place.

As I left Dr. Feel Alright's office, I couldn't stop thinking about that family portrait and how coincidental it was that the photographer had used a polarizing filter over the camera lens.

ohh mary

You were saving yourself for someone
who wouldn't create new civilizations in your bed.

You walked with evangelistic ease.

You weren't about to settle for the quiet life.

You told your fellow grads during your valedictorian speech,
"Today my still, pulsating heart beats
with papal innocence and tomboy heroism."

That summer you knocked the color
out of your lips and put a face gloss on you
to make it look like you were climbing trees.

"I want a gentler, softer image,"
you whispered to a dying perennial.
"I want to be romantic,
feminine and ironic as well."

Is that why you needed to find
a nice small place with a soul?

It's not so simple anymore.

That virginal sad-eyed sad sack
aesthetic no longer sells.

These days glamor comes
in that scary sequined way,
rooted in rhythm.

That entry in your journal scared me.

"Monday came like a porn star. A storm surge with the intensity of a
category 3 hurricane moved in with me, draping me in fireside bearskin

furs, leaving in its wake a super outbreak of gale force pain and paranoia. Funny how some events fall short of God's Original Plan."

It was an amazing high concept:

Lost girl befriends misfit/outcast and
the love and friendship that blooms
between them teaches them
important lessons.

You were the same
yesterday, today and forever.

You weren't some sort of make believe.

our styles just didn't coalesce

I will forever remember that cold morning.

I'd just returned from traveling cross-country in a beat-up Chevy on a month-long road trip in a quest for spiritual renewal.

She was in a state of absolute blah, standing by the picture window, looking typically unavailable, visibly moved by the leaves that were changing in the front yard.

"How were those long, lost hours in the Hollywood Hills?" she said.

"Like a platoon of soldiers searching for truth amidst an army of lies," I said.

"That's deep," she said, and gradually we slipped into some sort of shared psychosis.

"I've been doing some thinking," I said.

"Did it hurt?"

"You were right. I have given up on life. I need something to bring me back so I can start caring about something again. Where I really am or ever have been remains anyone's guess."

She shrugged. "That's the price you pay for living the life of the oblique mystic minstrel. Then tomorrow morning you'll wake up and tell me how bored you are and ask me how to resuscitate those facets of your personality that drive your creative spirit."

"My myth-telling surrealist poet days are over."

She laughed. "Actually, I've always found your tangled, impenetrable writings to be rather charming. In a self-aggrandizing, self-pitying sort of way."

I ignored that. "I wanna come back," I said.

She shook her head.

"I love you."

"There's only one man in my life right now and that's Jesus. He's the only man I can submit to, the only man who can teach me anything."

"I taught you how to make a whistle using bamboo."

"But you don't know how to teach me to be a better me. You can't teach me how to live in Christ and be built up in Him."

"How do you know?"

"Because you don't even like people. How do you expect to teach me how to live in Christ when you're such a misanthrope?"

"I'm not a misanthrope. I have some trust issues. Lemme tell you something, you want me to teach you to be a better you? I'll teach you how to be even *better* than a better you! While I was in Northern California, I went to this little motivational seminar where we all had to firewalk on hot stones as part of a test of our faith. You wanna be taught? Trust me, you'll learn a lot, very quickly. I'm serious; there was a very definite divine influence in those stones. I was transcended."

"Interesting how there are no references to firewalking in the bible."

"It could have been edited out, you don't know. There've been more revisions to The Bible than an Arnold Schwarzenegger script, for god's sakes. Look at all the translations. The interpretations. You can't even get a roomful of *scholars* to all agree. And you're gonna trust King James?"

"Yes, you know all the angles and you choose to stay on the outside. You choose."

"Because people like you continue to push me to the outside. All you people who wanna convert me."

"You push yourself. And I have never tried to convert you."

"It's the language you use. The nuances, the subtleties. That superior sort of holier-than-thou… that personal relationship you have with Jesus. How you're going to heaven because you have that relationship and I'm not because I'm a Jew and I don't live in Christ."

"You're crazy."

"And you're a bigot!"

I don't remember anything else that was said that morning. But I remember that slap. And I remember her eyes welling up and I remember those broken sobs.

And I remember driving home, without any heat, while a few pattering drops of rain came down, followed by snow and sleet.

When the phone rang at noon the following day, the voice at the other end said, "I forgive you for calling me a bigot."

I said, "I love you."

The voice said, "I love you, too."

this notion of participation

I just never applied myself.

I'd draw pictures in my notebook.

Pictures of super heroes and their weapons of mass destruction.

(But at least they never lied about having them).

Sometimes my teachers would call on me.
Sometimes I'd answer them.
But mostly I'd stare out the window.
Watching the janitors mowing the lawn.
Raking up the leaves.
Smiling cynically at the first-year teachers.

I wasn't bored.

Or maybe I was and just didn't realize it.

Between classes I'd smoke in the boy's room.
Swapping stories about my past with
all the other underachievers.

Then get busted.
Usually by a gym teacher wearing a sweat suit and
a whistle around their neck all day.

"You kids better get a clue! No one's givin' out
diplomas in the boy's room. Get outta here!"

We'd scatter.
Wondering what our next move was going to be.
Our guts squirming.
Our butts soar from sitting in detention hall all day.

It was a lousy place to network,
but a great place to be indifferent.

During study hall, I'd sit in the band room.
Drawing.
Mr. O'Leary, the band director,
would walk in and out of his office all morning.
Red-faced.
Puffing out his cheeks.
Smelling of stale smoke.
Whistling the first trumpet part
to the William Tell Overture.
Sometimes he'd see me and nod.
I'd nod back.
He'd go back into his office.
Continue working on his latest composition.
"Ode to a Middle-aged Man Trying to Bring an
Understanding of the Human Being to the World."

Most of the kids just laughed at his red face.
His paunch. And his bald head.

But even then I understood we all have different colors in us
and gave the guy half a break.

Even though he flunked me for Music Appreciation.

"I don't play any Black Sabbath in here,"
he told us on the first day of class.

"How about Leonard Cohen?" somebody shot back.

"Who?"

We all laughed.

He got flustered.

And sent all ten of us to the principal's office.

"Why are you all here?" the principal said.

"Because Mr. O'Leary doesn't know who Leonard Cohen is," somebody
said.

"Who's Leonard Cohen?" the principal said.

We all laughed.

So did the principal.

That's why we liked him.

He could take a joke and swallow it whole.

We also liked him because he never held back
his frustrations with some of our teachers,
especially Mr. O'Leary.

"Frank's just pissed because we cut the budget again
for the music department… he doesn't understand,
people wanna see football, not listen to some
John Philip Sousa marching band music, for God's sakes…
go on, go back to class. And tell him if he ever sends his
whole class to me again… never mind."

By the time we got back to the band room,
Mr. O'Leary had locked us out.

So we all went outside to smoke cigarettes and
take turns reading passages from Leonard Cohen's
"Beautiful Losers"
while Mr. O'Leary slept in his office,
stuck with a modest array of talent.

our absence from life

I was in Penn Station waiting for the train to take me to New Haven. I was sitting by myself, away from the crowd, reading something by John Paul Sartre. "No Exit", I think. I couldn't really concentrate on the words; they were demanding too much of me. My mind kept drifting. I'd just been fired. I was working in a photographic lab. I came across some nude photos of a famous entertainer. I started showing them to my coworkers. Somebody ratted on me.

A woman appeared. First thing I noticed about her was her hair. Like a Fraggle. And she had a lazy eye. It kept drifting over toward the bridge of her nose every now and then. She'd tried glasses, contacts, nothing helped. So she just resigned herself to the fact that her eye was going to be drifting over toward the bridge of her nose every now and then. "What's funny," she said. "Is people are usually more concerned about it than I am." And that really rang true to me. I told her to have a seat, but she said she'd been sitting all day. She worked for a bank as a data entry operator and said it felt good to stand, for a change.

"I had too many errors this month... my supervisor took me into his office and said if I didn't cut down on my errors, he was gonna have to let me go."

"Funny how supervisors are," I said.

She smiled and shook her head. "Bein' human really hurts sometimes, doesn't it?"

"It's only natural," I said.

"Where are you going?"

"New Haven."

"What's in New Haven?"

"My parents."

"Visiting?"

I waited a few seconds before answering that one because I wasn't sure why I was going back home. I had a feeling I was going there to hide, but I didn't want to tell her that, so I gave her a bullshit answer. "My sister's getting married."

"How wonderful," she said.

I shrugged. "I guess."

"You guess?" she said.

"It was very sudden."

"Ohh?"

"She just met him a month ago... he's a musician... he's on the road... that's gonna be their life... not that that's..."

"I understand," she said.

I watched her eye wandering around like a marble in a glass of milk. She was actually kind of attractive, if you could get pass that slothful eye. She had a real nice body. Pretty feet; the polish on her toenails was chipping, but I found that kind of sexy. I've always been attracted to women who are slowly ripping apart at the seams, and don't have the energy to sew themselves back together again.

"Are you married?" she said.

I shook my head.

"Ever been married?"

I shook my head again.

"It's not for everyone," she said. "I thought it was for me... till one day I realized I hated having to compromise like that all the time... with marriage, you constantly have to take the other person's feelings into consideration... and I'm just too self-indulgent!" She laughed. "Plus my husband's..." She stopped herself, but only for a second. "Gay..."

"Gay?"

She looked really embarrassed. I restrained myself from asking her about a dozen and a half more questions.

"I had my suspicions before we got married," she said. "I noticed it would take him a long time to..." She stopped herself again, looking around, making sure nobody overheard her, and whispered carefully, "become aroused... I mean, I can usually arouse a guy like that." She snapped her fingers proudly, but quickly realized what she had just said and covered her mouth with a few of her fingers. "Oops! Too much information? I'm usually not this high self-disclosing... it's just that you're so quiet and silence intimidates me..."

"I'm not trying to intimidate you," I said. "I'm just listening."

She looked at me for a minute. "You have patient eyes," she said. "Very welcoming eyes."

"Thank you."

"My name's Melba. I'm going to Philadelphia. I think... I have a sister there. We don't get along at all... I just need to get away for a while... she said I could stay with her for a week... Oh, I have been so stressed lately... between discovering my husband's gay and my shitty job and my creditors and... I just got a call from one of them the other day... I totally blanked on this one debt I owed for like nine thousand dollars... imagine forgetting about nine thousand dollars... but somehow, six years later, their little skip tracers tracked me down... I think if it had gone another year it would have dropped off my credit report... oh well... gotta pay the piper eventually, I suppose... Why do gay men marry straight women? What was he preserving and protecting himself from? He was a *barista*, for God's sakes! He made coffee and tea! It's not like he had a career to protect or anything! Half the people that worked there were gay! 'Course, my family is so incredibly homophobic. Now it makes sense, but why would he have even considered marriage? What was he thinking? What was the point? And why me? What was it about me that? You know what? I need to stop. I cannot keep doing this to myself. It's over. Oprah would tell me it's over. He ran off with some actor who was supposedly some producer's third or fourth choice for 'Queer Eye for the Straight Guy' and I'm sitting in Penn Station about to take a train to my overachieving, anal retentive public defender sister whose conservative Christian Republican husband was just elected to the state senate, whose three naturally curly blond children are all enrolled in a Montessori school... and what the hell am I going to do with the rest of my fucking life?" She started to cry, then reached into her purse and pulled out one of those bandanas, the kind I used to tie around my head in junior high, and wiped away some of her tears. "I read someplace there are like four basic questions in life," she said, blotting the corner of her left eye with the bandana. "Who am I? Do you believe in God? Do you love me? And where do we go?" She shrugged, "You know, after we die... at this point, I don't know and don't care... I'm sorry for unloading all my psychic bile on you like this..."

"It's okay," I said.

"Every day's been high-pitched. Dramatic. And I don't like it. It's the truth..."

"I understand."

We heard a voice over the public address system announcing that the train to Philadelphia was now boarding.

"Oh my goodness, that's me," she said, grabbing her bags. She took a deep breath. "I can do this...I can definitely do this..."

"Yes, you can," I said.

I could tell she was touched. "Thank you for saying that... I've had so precious little positive re-enforcement in my life lately... it's been like nothing but false starts and broken hearts..."

I nodded and smiled.

"It's really true," she said, pausing for a second or two. "...I appreciate it..." She turned and walked toward the platform.
When I arrived in New Haven, I took a cab to my parents' house.

As we pulled into the drive, I just sat there, staring at the front door.

The cabby turned around to check on me. "Ya alright, kid?" he said.

I waited. "…I think I'm gonna check into a motel tonight instead…"

the requiem of this man's spirit

At night I hear the taunting, haunting
voices shouting in my sleep.
I am atrophying, paralyzed.
I think of the inquiring Hamlet,
the misanthropic Steppenwolf,
and my own weary father,
a self-described ne'er do well
who painted parking spaces for a living and
was the only registered socialist in town.

These daring men of failure shared the
onerous responsibility of having to
reconcile their own morbid sensitivities and
profound self-contempt with a world that
eschews such masculine displays of dis-ease.

I too live the double life of
Performer and Critic;
too involved with my own ego,
unable to synthesize my unconscious with
my conscious.

I act with arrogance and pride as I live
among the people,
am tempted by desires of the flesh,
imbibe a variety of spirits,
indulge in richly-tasting foods,
practice vanity, haste, impatience, and excess
and hold any man who possesses less than I in
contempt and reproach him for committing
the sin of sloth.

to leave the consideration of the self behind

She was into Goth and blood play,
walked around in black t-shirts
that said "Wholesale Slut,"
admitted to having a jones for
the Osmonds,
never allowed a man
with a memory
to share her bed.

In high school she was voted
most likely to be involved
in a tabloid scandal.

In college
she only dated
black guys.

In graduate school
she decided not to
become a registered voter.

Her journals were filled
with entries like:

"The world is my oyster and
it just gave me a bacterial infection,"
and
"Between sex and love,
I would choose nothing."

Word on the street was that she
behaved admirably in the company
of archbishops and historians
though not so stellar in the presence
of philanthropists and diplomats.

I was in shul the day
she was bat mitzvahed
on her 30th birthday.
She wore a black leather yarmulke,
a cape covered with little
sequined Star of Davids',
accompanied by a goth metal band
during the reading of her Haftorah.

On the day of her funeral,
we all played hooky from work,
walked around barefoot,
got snookered on absinthe and
behaved as if we were
in the company
of philanthropists and diplomats.

But we all agreed
that when she made
the covers of
Time and Newsweek
the following week
that she had had
too many dates
with strangers and not
enough blood play
with archbishops and historians.

quicksilver goddess

History's most misunderstood woman
smiles softly in the shadows
of a silent Sunday,
chafed from being a
refugee from responsibility.

She's afraid she's not
much of a hit with men.

She doesn't laugh at their jokes.

She doesn't find most of what
they say particularly funny.

She finds it irksome.

Although she laughs at Hamlet.

Those who know her well say
her silences are more eloquent
than her spoken word.

And those who know her
peripherally
say she rolls her eyes too much
whenever she's frustrated.

She doesn't care,
though,
on this silent Sunday
because she's sprawled
across her bed,
relaxed with pep,
waiting for someone
to lye next to and
searching for a balance
between brutality and banality

with both eyes closed.

truth arrested

Daisy's session with Dr. Gould began a few minutes late.

"Sometimes," she said. "I go out in public without my glasses so that if I have to look people in the eye I don't really see them... I'm not so inhibited around them when I do this..."

Dr. Gould nodded.

Daisy reached into her pocketbook and pulled out an index card. "May I read you something?" she said.

"Of course."

"I wrote it last night... I call it 'Things I've Learned. I've learned it's not always necessary to defend myself. I've learned to leave people alone. I've learned that no matter how much support, encouragement, and education you may give to someone, they may not always rise above their own circumstances. I've learned that a lack of motivation in a man will force him into becoming a confirmed bachelor for the rest of his life.'"

Daisy continued staring at the card, even though she had finished reading from it.

After about 30 seconds of silence, Gould nodded and said, "That's very penetrating... How is Ethan?"

"My boyfriend's name is Efren."

"Sorry."

"We had one of our marathon talks the other night. I told him he needed someone to be his hero. He broke down and curled up into the fetal position. He was crying so hard he was hyperventilating. I got very scared for him... I told him he was going to have to find a job soon or else..." She trailed off.

"Or else..."

Daisy began cleaning her finger nails with the edge of the index card.

"Or else I would have to get a third job," she said.

"You didn't say that," Dr. Gould said.

"No... I didn't..."

"But you thought it."

Daisy was silent for a moment. "Yes..."

She turned the card over. "I wrote something else..."

"I'd like to hear it."

"'Every kiss begins with negotiations. After negotiations comes compromise. After compromise comes victory. After victory comes the transition of power. After the transition of power comes complacency. After complacency comes the separation of feelings. After the separation of feelings comes...'" She stopped and shrugged. "That was it," she said. "I couldn't think of anything else to write..."

"May I see that?"

She handed the card to Gould. He read both sides, handed it back to her, said, "Tell me what Ethan-"

"Efren."

"Right. Tell me again why he appeals to you?"

Daisy laid her head back, closed her eyes, sighed. "He doesn't take any shit from me... I can't be with a man who takes my shit..."

Just then, Gould's watch alarm went off, signaling an end to Daisy's session.

As she left the office and walked outside, she removed her glasses and put them in a case in her purse.

That's when it came to her.

After the separation of feelings, she thought, comes the rest of your life.

following you to the re-beginnings of the earth

I

My ego was on fire,
I believed,
I perceived
I was well-thought of
in certain squares,
even the occasional triangle,
but nobody ever let me into
the circles,
they told me I wasn't well-rounded enough,
my style lacked panache,
I didn't get a degree in something that
made me stand out,
my degree was in sitting-down.
I enrolled the year after the final commencement,
but very few people ever noticed me in class.
I handed in all my assignments,
but didn't receive a grade.
I was a holy ghost of a different kind,
who left behind a scent of money
that couldn't buy class.

II

I wondered where I'd be
when the four horses of the apocalypse
rode into town,
into the sundown,
the night shining in armor,
it's all there,
in black and white,
in African American and Caucasian,
the writing is on the floor;
it fell off the wall,

now everybody's walkin' all over
the words and smudging them and
now nobody knows what the fuck's going on,
they're just praying to
gods unseen and gods unclean.
They don't know about reciprocity
or the eventual downfall of theocracy,
they've been to the meetings and joined in
on the hymns, but their voices are so hoarse,
they can never hit that high C, man,
they're always struggling to come to terms
with that high C,
so they compromise,
which is the worst thing you can do
in a situation like that,
they go down an octave, and that really
diminishes the power,
the point of it all,
so the congregation is left for dead and
not for resurrection,
even though the insurrection
has just begun.

perfect, like a fairy tale

I asked you to marry me on that Ferris wheel at Coney Island.

You couldn't stop laughing.

You got me an Hawaiian shirt and a
fifty dollar gift certificate to 7-Eleven
for my fortieth birthday and then fell asleep
after I blew out all the candles on my birthday cake.

I later found out you bought a Sara Lee Pound Cake
and used the filling from Devil Dogs as frosting.

So I got drunk on Bloody Matadors and drove to
Worcester, Mass.

Got some Chinese symbols tattooed on my chest.
Had very little to eat for the next day and a half.

When I called you collect from that flooded phone booth
near the Centrum,
you told the operator you were sorry
but you thought I had died.

Six months later I read in the newspaper
that your father had been investigated
by the SEC and was going to jail for
doing funny things with
other people's money and I knew you needed a friend.

When you answered the phone, you were drunk.

Drunk and alone, sitting in the dark, listening to Cat Stevens.

"You live and learn," you said.

That was the only thing you said.

We stayed on the phone,
not talking,
just listening to Cat.

I fell asleep, still connected.

a very chilled-out experience

The room was filled with tattoos, dreds, torn clothing, stiletto boots.

Lotta confusion.

Lotta tectonic plate shifting going on.

A California Kid mumbled something about environmental politics, then got on his cell phone.

A Familiar Spirit with bunched-up panties and a booby bra shifted in her chair and flashed a Kool-Aid smile at the California Kid.

The Kid, whose long, bushy eye brows added ten years to his face, folded his phone and placed it in his knapsack.

"I don't believe we've been introduced," he said, with plenty of asexual tension.

The Familiar Spirit was unflappable. "Don't have a handle on your Dionysian spirit, do you?"

"My what?"

"Your tendency toward drunken and orgiastic behavior… after the Greek God Dionysus."

"Oh really?"

There was a pause that would have pleased Pinter.

Then the Familiar Spirit opened a pack of unfiltered Pall Malls. For a millisecond she thought about offering the Kid one, or even a drag from it, but instead decided to save them for her birthday.

"You're straying too far from your personal truth," she said, lighting the butt.

The Kid cocked his head defiantly. "Oh really?"

"It's those weird noises you make… they mean you don't give a damn."

The Kid, who usually had complete confidence in his abilities, was feeling a bit piqued at the moment; the last 3 minutes of his life had been completely drained from him and he was desperately trying to figure out how the hell to get them back.

"Well," he said. "I'm still here… I'm like a bad stain, man… I'm the same kid I was in the sandbox in 1968…" He hesitated, then added. "It's memory that matters."

The Familiar Spirit took a long drag from the cigarette, blew the smoke toward the equator. "Well, that more or less defines O.T.T., donchya think?"

The Kid's eyebrows narrowed.

"Over the top," the Familiar Spirit said, brushing ashes from her lap.

The Kid thought about becoming hostile for a minute, but he reminded himself he was a Buddhist. Well, he was sort of a Buddhist. At least he had an appreciation for Buddhism. Which was better than not being one at all.

"Are you not enjoying yourself?" the Familiar Spirit said.

The Kid folded his arms.

The Familiar Spirit nodded.

That was the moment we all looked at each other and welled-up in the eyes.

a sort of separation

I find myself being less and less engaged in conversations.

People will tell me all about their trips to Italy,
their friends who call them at two
in the morning to tell them their troubles,
how they've got a couple days' vacation coming to them and
they're going to spend it rearranging their closets.

They'll tell me about their sons and daughters,
how they're just like all the others;
on their tenth job,
hooked on Ecstasy,
going into the army,
flunking out of community college,
hitchhiking to Alaska,
worshiping false idols.

And then I'll yawn or suddenly remember to change the
air filter in my car or think about how easy
it would be to just drop out of society and
become dependent on welfare.

Then I'll hear them say something like,
"Gosh, what can I wear that's flattering?"
or "And all the congregation lifted up their
voice and cried; and the people wept that night,"
and my eyes will glaze over and I'll start to doze off.

And then I'll hear, "Are you listening to me?"

"Of course, of course," I'll say,
hoping they won't ask me to repeat what they've just said.

I'm amazed these people still consider me a friend.

If they knew just how little I really listen to them.

They'd probably re-evaluate our friendship.

And I'd be alone.

Again…

trying to laugh at myself without making the audience feel uncomfortable

I looked out the window and saw the moon rising behind the Observatory and thought maybe this time I had a chance. I could rise above my circumstances, turn things around, make something happen for myself.

I poured myself another cup of coffee, sweetened it with Bailey's Irish Cream, thought about avoiding the appearance of idleness, but balked at the idea, choosing to take a walk instead.

As I locked the door behind me, I was accosted by that fuzzy old lady in 2B who'd fallen into a few too many traps in her life and thought of me (sarcastically) as a new breed of warrior poet.

"Well, well…been setting anymore fires you can't put out?" she said.

"No, but I've rededicated my life to Jesus."

She looked at me like she was watching CSPAN at three in the morning. "I wouldn't exactly brag about that, if I were you."

"Good thing is, you're not me."

I walked outside into the bitter chill. Channel 3's chief meteorologist said it was twenty-one degrees with winds gusting to thirty miles per hour, but I just ignored it, and worked my way west toward the brilliant sky.

I heard a voice singing in the distance. It was thin and reedy and it reminded me of a pretty bitter memory.

And then my mobile rang. It was Jaqué, a tired-out chick I'd met during my sanctified period who was always looking to me for mercy whenever the going got rough.

"What now, Jaqué?"

"That's no way to treat a lady," Jaqué said.

"Maybe not, but it's how I treat you."

"Meany."

"You know I'm nuts about you," I said. "Long as you're living in another state."

"I moved," Jaqué said.

"You're not in ATL, anymore?"

"Too much like Houston."

"What happened?"

"Well, it's a long story," Jaqué said. "But the school I was working for? Turns out they were never accredited. So the state shut 'em down."

"Jeeez."

"So I'm here…at the Courtyard."

"Marriot?" I said.

"Yuppers."

"Mmm."

There was a really long pause.

"We don't have to see each other if you don't wanna," Jaqué said.

"No?"

"Well, I mean, I'm not gonna beg you for a booty call, but it'd be nice…" She waited. "Wouldn't it?"

This time I waited.

"Unless you're seeing someone?" Jaqué said.

I waited even longer.

"Are you?"

"Technically, no," I said.

"Lemme guess. You're seeing someone who wants a definition of the relationship, but you're not ready to give her a definition, so things are pretty much up in the air?"

I was about to hang up on her, when I got another call.

"Hold on," I said.

"Please don't put me on hol-"

I answered the other call. "Hello?"

"Hey, sweetie pie honey bunch."

It was Frieda, the girl whom I was technically not seeing.

"Hey," I said.

"Whucha doin'?" she said.

"Nothin' worth mentioning."

"Whucha doin' tonight?"

"Figured I'd begin that journey of a thousand steps," I said.

"Oh yeah? I've been workin' out on the stair stepper a lot lately. New Year's resolution and all."

That's what I loved about Frieda; the way her mind worked.

"So who's on the other line?" Frieda said.

I hated my call waiting; people could always tell I was on another call whenever I answered the other line because of the weird clicking sounds it always made. Like somebody tap dancing on cracked linoleum.

"No one important," I said.

"Are you bullshitting me again?" Frieda said.

"Again?"

"You are."

"Why would you say that?"

"Because I know you."

"I'm not."

Frieda giggled.

"I gotta go," I said.

"Give her my love."

I disconnected Frieda and returned to Jaqué.

"I'm back," I said.

"I know," Jaqué said. "You're interesting that way."

"Hmm?"

"Nothing," Jaqué said. "I'm a little discombobulated...I just took some Valium..."

"*Some?*"

"*A* Valium."

"You said *some.*"

"I misspoke."

"Are you sure?"

"*Yes!*…God, you treat me like a friggin' drug addict."

I let that remark hang in the air.

"Alright, well, lemme go find my little Jack Rabbit," Jaqué said.

I told her I'd be there in a few minutes.

Jaqué groaned. "That sounded so obligatory…You know, I always told myself, the next guy I fall in love with is literally gonna have to come up to me and say, 'I am from God, you are my rib'… But look at me these days, man…settlin' for 'I'll be there in a few minutes'…why can't I just be content with a little solitude?"

"Cuz solitude's like a cranky woman who keeps pleading with you to be kind to her," I said.

"You think you're so smart," Jaqué said. "But, baby, you've met your match."

I hung up, jumped in a cab, told the driver to take his time in getting there.

"No point in rushing things," I mumbled, settling into another of my passive silences.

how can i possibly put the last two years of my life with you into words?

It was back a few years. 1992, 1994, somewhere round there.

I'd suddenly become haggard, emotionally worn, and disillusioned, virtually overnight. The young lady, whom I was dating at the time, had scribbled something on the front and back of an envelope and left it on my pillow just before taking an overdose of her father's heart medication.

"There are a lot of people out there who pretend to have all the answers. If I could make them feel the way I feel during the lowest of my lows for one week. Just one week, that would be the sweetest revenge I could ever imagine because there are a lot of people out there who think I'm just crying victim here. That I'm weak. I didn't have the fortitude to bounce back and get my second wind in life because I wasn't strong enough to deal with the disappointments, the shortcomings, the setbacks, the bad breaks! I mean, what do they, honestly think that this shit is just a figment of my imagination? That it's just a mild case of the blahs? We're all looking for the perfect respite to the monotonous life, but it becomes more difficult as we slightly age and lose that twinkle in our eyes, no matter how much we attempt to block out any semblance of reality. Why go through life dissatisfied and complacent? Why keep sighing into our martinis late into the night and becoming copies of the people next to us? Why turn to music to express our suppressed feelings and thoughts and emotions when we really should be turning to each other? And why, at this point, even attempt to create a story of friendship and hope amid such a dismal tableau?"

When you read a note like that in a book or in a newspaper or hear a character in a movie or a play says it you think, "Oh, how sad, how pervasive, how inescapable, what a tragedy."

But when it's written by someone you love, who knows you're a down-and-out guy with trust issues, you don't think how sad or painful or tragic it is. You just think, but I thought we had this all worked-out? And then you think, what about the engagement ring I just bought? And then you think, I'm sorry I was a bit absent, I was just trying to find the courage and the energy.   And then you tell yourself to stop thinking because what you're thinking doesn't really represent what you're trying to say.

So you fold the envelope, stick it in the top left bureau drawer next to a digital thermometer and a box of Benadryl and a shot glass that says Savannah Georgia on it and two spare keys from an old Toyota pickup truck and a pair of left-handed scissors and a yellow highlighter and your checkbook and an empty pill vial and a bottle of rosemary mint body cleanser and you close the drawer, drink a light scotch and soda, lye back down on your bed and the phone rings and you answer it and a voice on the other end says, "She's gonna be okay.   They had to pump her stomach, she's lying comfortably now, she's gonna be alright," and you say, "Thank God," and you hang up and you think, why do I always fall in love with women who seem to have no interest in me?

thrift shop princesses

Zoë Fluck and Chloe Zuck
were always partying sober,
tanning in the summer
but never getting their makeup
to look good.

When Zoë had a breakdown
during an autumnal equinox,
(she went to bed and just stayed
there for a couple weeks),
Chloe was regularly seen
Novocaine-faced,
lounging in big baggy pants, and
wearing colored contacts that felt
like little metal Frisbees.

The day Zoë finally got Chloe
on the phone,
their conversation was clearly
from the unconscious.

"I had a dream," Zoë said.

"Oh, God," Chloe said.
"I hate it when people retell their dreams."

"No, you'll appreciate this one.
I was wearing big white fur pants and
my father kept telling me
I was sexually ambiguous..."

"Well," Chloe said.
"I read a book that said if we sleep
in a certain direction facing the moon,
it helps us to achieve amazing new
depth or breadth or some bullshit..."

It was April before Zoë and Chloe
were back to their usual hooliganism,
walking around in big corduroy overcoats,
funky hats and really tight flannel pants, and
taking pot shots at Orange County.

in the confession season

On a retreat,
somewhere in the Berkshires,
someone served us batter cakes
with blackberry brandy syrup
and I swear there was a coffin in
the middle of the living room
being used as a coffee table.

When I asked the mistress of the
house if this was true,
she put her index finger to her lips
and hushed me.

"Plenty of time for that," she said.
"Plenty of time. Let's play Twister!"

Last time I'd played Twister,
I ended up in the hospital with a
herniated disc so I politely declined
the invitation and retired to an
upstairs bedroom with clapboard
floors and aluminum siding walls.

Before I could settle into one of the
many hemp bean bag chairs,
(they felt like they were stuffed
with ball bearings),
the doorbell rang.

It took me a minute to realize that
it was the doorbell to my door,
not the front door,
so I opened it.

It was Serena,
a friend of mine from
the New School,

who was smiling like the
Dalai Lama and looking
fashionably frugal in a dress she'd
recently made out of muslin sheets.

"I think I forgot to tell you…"
Her words faded away.
She withdrew.
Became suddenly shy,
which was unusual for Serena.

I cupped her left breast,
held it in my hand
and said,
"It's alright, Serena, you can do it."

Her head drooped.

She turned off her eyes.

"What is it, Serena?" I said.

She scratched the middle knuckle
on her right hand
so hard, she drew blood.

"I used to give half a shit," she whispered.
"'Course, this was years ago…when I was
young and rambunctious…and far less
irritable…now everything is just so…"

Her left shoulder began to twitch.

"…Perfunctory…obligatory…
I know I've kept a pretty low profile lately…
But I've been good for you, haven't I?
Mostly? On average?"

"Of course," I said.

She nodded. And seemed relieved.

"Well, that's grand," she said. "I'm glad
we can be so intensely personal with
each other."

She touched my lips with the peace sign.

My glasses began to fog up.

"Isn't coalescence a gift?" she said.

I was perspiring.

"Would you like to come in?" I said.

She paused,
slowly shook her head.

"I haven't meditated all day," she said
"And I'm feeling very raddled,"
and then she turned to leave.

As she walked down the hall, she
chanted something inaudible.

I could suddenly hear my carotid artery
carrying blood to my head.

I got sleepy.

And for some reason felt remorseful.

I collapsed into a ball on the bed,
closed my eyes and tried
to remember what kind of medication
I was on.

In another room, on another floor,
Serena sat gracefully,
in full lotus position,
looking like a watercolor daydream.

the old morality was still hanging around

Hannah Morgenstern was the most
succinct example of instant karma
I'd ever known.

In seventh grade, she handed me a book
during recess entitled,
"A Search for the Proper Discipline."

When I asked her what it was about,
she said, "Rage, toil, guilt and boredom."

As she walked away,
she seduced the wind
with her hair and
colored herself a blue funk.

I opened the book about midway through and began reading.

"I realized I was going to have to find a faraway place where nobody could
talk to me. I'd bring along a tape recorder, of course, to record the sounds
of an attic room somewhere far above the train station where I would jot
down my observations of ashes curling up and taking a power nap in a
recent urn. I'd have no alarm clock to reunite with, no bellowing voice
announcing my mortality, simply a gentle breeze squeezing through a
keyhole of a locked door at the end of a hallway to greet me. Naturally,
there would be a synagogue mouse there, they're always there, and maybe
even an indifferent, yawning feline..."

Then the bell rang,
signaling an end to recess.

I closed the book, and went inside
to give the book back to
Hannah Morgenstern,
but she wasn't at her desk.

"Where's Hannah?" I asked Rachel, her best friend.

"Her mom picked her up," Rachel said.

"Is she sick?"

"No, she's moving to New Mexico."

"How come?"

Rachel shrugged.

I sat down at my desk,
opened the book to the last page and
read the final paragraph.

"Half-shy, half-arrogant, I awoke in the middle of the night with the cold
sweats, the hot flashes, and the ugly truth taking over. It wasn't until two
o'clock the following day before I began to renew my faith in the power of
the delicate high wire act which was my life. Unable to hold my peace any
longer, I sat alone, near a picture window, nostalgic for my boyhood,
listening to my instincts, and the mice building shelter behind those
gloomy walls. I got up, lit a cigarette, had some gin, noticed the thinning
rug beneath my callous soles, and called out to the jangled young woman
in the next room, studying for a mail order course which would one day
earn her an associates degree in paralegal studies. Laughter was simply
out of the question for me. The only thing I found even remotely
humorous was my Lord, my Savior. 'It is finished.' (The greatest one liner
in comedy history)."

very thinly and comically disguised

Rappin' with this dude named Ty from Soho;
he's an artist,
a painter,
an observer of the human condition and
other pretentious phases and phrases.

He listens to Coltrane by the light
of a black light as he slaps multicultural
swaths of color and texture across his life's
canvas and smokes a doobie the size of a
stogie and creates angry bitter satire,
ironic and sardonic images designed to
mask his psychopathic preoccupations.

I like to engage Ty in discourses on
politics and sociology, religion and philosophy,
because his rejoinders are so hip and cryptic,
his delivery so razor-sharp,
his thoughts so intuitive and insightful,
I end up questioning everything I believe in.

I ask him if he believes in God, he says,
"If he believes in me,"
which on the surface seems so facile,
so cheeky,
so Dylanesque.

But as I reflect further
on this statement and delve
deeper into its content,
I sense a certain sadness and poignancy,
longing and desire as well as a hint of hopelessness and despair.

When I challenge his logic,
he recoils and smiles sheepishly,
as if I have caught him in a lie.
He shrugs and avoids my eyes and

begins humming a Pink Floyd tune,
the one about feeling comfortably numb,
and immediately bursts into mirthful laughter,
mumbling something about him being
"experienced like Jimi…"

I pause and inhale his breath and
wonder when he will come out
of his depression.

"Life is so non-linear and haphazard and
random and yet,"
he swallows and chokes simultaneously,
but remains steadfast in his ability
to finish the thought.
"And yet there's such a pattern,
a coherence,
almost an anal/oral quality to it all,
I almost have to believe in something
larger than myself."

This is the closest I have ever heard him
come to acknowledgment and acceptance.

He has lived half his life quoting
Camus and Sartre and Marx and Heidegger and
prides himself on his non-beliefs in everything from
a higher being to the American dream and is practically
sadistic in his treatment of those that are loyal and devout,
idealistic and patriotic,
in love and in matrimony;
the two are always mutually-exclusive to him.

For the first time I feel his existential foundation
beginning to crack.

However, my respect for his sensibility and
my compassion for his failures as a man preclude me
from destroying the structure he has so diligently
tried to construct,
to code or not to code, that is the question.

And so we sit together
in a comfortable silence,
complacent and fat,
lonely and at peace,
wondering why our conversations lag and
why we allow confrontations to go unchallenged.

it's never boring though i'm not sure it has a point

On Tuesday, July 2, 1995, I was parked in a car at the top of a hill with a gun and a bottle of Xanex.

I began thinking about all those broken pieces I didn't know how to fix that made me behave a certain way and suddenly I could feel all that shame manifesting itself into anger and hardness and I knew if those feelings gathered enough force, the little guy with the hatchet that lives inside of me would wake up and begin chipping away at all that old stuff from my childhood and then I'd probably pick up at that gun and...

That's when I knew I was heading toward a place I didn't want to go and it was time to put my life back together.

And then I remembered something you told me years ago, long before I began pretending to be who I am today.

"No matter who you are or what you do, you will be assimilated into a society that will not tolerate rebellion... you are compromised, or you die...there's no way to win."

Yeah, you knew how to play the game and tried in vain to explain most of the rules to me, but, as usual, I didn't listen.

I was sneaking off for a long smoke with one of those bad influences you were always warning me about or negotiating with the virgin next door or attempting to teach myself to play the drums or fishing for trout in that stream in back of our house or laughing at anybody older than twenty-five.

Then a funny thing happened.

I turned twenty-six.

And I wondered how the hell a thing like that could have ever happened to a guy like me.

Not that I ever thought I'd be immortal.

I just figured somehow I'd be able to put up a better fight than most.

But I soon realized that even the best of fighters are subject to chronic brain damage as a result of the repeated pummeling they take from the establishment for violating their norms, and I never factored that part of it into the equation, which shouldn't surprise you.

Not that I was looking for a revolution.

You know I never cared about being socially conscious.

Just wanted to divide my time between holding the exhaustion and self-pity at bay and trying not to become another archetype of the tragic soul.

If it appeared as if I had nothing on my mind in particular, it was only because I was trying to find a comfortable way of absolving myself of responsibility.

I guess you kind of get like that when you're eager to forget your sorrows.

And so I ended up in some really funky, fantastical places with some really grimy and feral-looking punks who'd suffered some really dramatic bruises to their global images, just like me.

Things were always bubbling up from some crazy, naughty place inside of me that I was completely unprepared for and most days I was so distracted, I couldn't even think, so I just stared blankly and spoke slowly and softly, if I spoke at all.

I now realize I was finding the distance from what was painful; those very sad adolescent wounds take so long to heal.

Even after all these years, I'm still trying to resolve my master plot: an erring person making serious mistakes and secretly trying to live down their consequences recognizes the foolishness of attempting to be other than one's true self.

I work on resolving it every day.

Because the little guy with the hatchet still lives inside of me, and he's sleeping now.

I don't want him to ever wake up again.

his indestructible human spirit

He wanted to know what I did in my spare time; told him I do a little writing here and there.

"So you drink much or...?" he said.

"Do I drink much?"

"I know a lotta writers drink. I was just curious."

"I mean, occasionally."

"Nothin' like Hemingway, though, right? I mean *he* was a *drinker*. Believed life was a tragedy and knew it could only have one end."

"That's right."

"Had high cholesterol and high blood pressure and an aorta inflammation."

"I didn't know that."

"Mm hmm. Died July 27th, 1961, five AM from a self-inflicted gunshot blast to the head. You're not that conflicted, are ya?"

"I don't think so."

"Ya think the more conflicted a writer is the more talented they are, or...?"

"Not necessarily."

"Ya think mental illness diminishes or enhances a writer's ability?"

"I have no way of even..."

"Yeah, I do a little writing myself."

"Oh yeah?"

"Just some poetry, you know, short stories, nothin' major. I'm totally into Shakespeare. I mean, if you gotta have a writer as a role model, ya know what I mean? Like he frames everything I write and how I live my life. Like whenever I'm describing a character, tryna get it right, in my mind, I'm linkin' them to, like Iago or Hamlet or Ophelia or Macbeth or Lear, you know, it helps me to structure my own characters...'course, Shakespeare stole many of his plots from the Greeks. Or was it Christopher Marlowe? Marlowe was killed in a tavern brawl on May 30, 1593."

"Really..."

"Yeah. Hamlet was an interesting character. I essentially agree with him when he says, you know, that basically life's a piece of shit 'cause there are so many assholes out there makin' it so fucken unbearable for us, so what's the point? And I suppose a lotta people would say his saving grace is that he *doesn't* off himself...'cause he says, what does he say? 'Something after death' could be worse? Somethin' like that? Anyway, I dunno, who knows? Whatever, right?"

"Mm, interesting..."

"Yeah. Well, very cool. Always good to run into a fellow scribe..." He checked his watch. "Yo, I'm late for my shock therapy session. Lot of things goin' on with me emotionally. Workin through 'em though, with the help of my savior, yo," and he gave a thumbs up.

"That's good news for you," I said.

"It is, definitely, God is good. But ya know what I've learned?"

"What's that?"

"A lot of defining moments that build or break your character happen in a blink of an eye," and he let that one hang in the air for a while. "Well, good luck, man, keep writing. You know, sometimes it's all we have..."

He walked away, whistling.

I walked away, unable to blink my eyes.

the short bus

Guy came up to me at the bus stop, wanting to know why my arms were folded.

"You know what kinda nonverbal communication you're sendin' off by keepin' your arms all folded like that?"

"No," I said.

"You're a closed-up individual."

Then, demonstrating my body language, he said, "This here says, 'I want nothin' to do with you 'cause I'm better than you,' and that's what you're very subtly tryin' to communicate to me."

"Really?"

"That's right..."

"Ohh..."

"Don't let nobody in. Keep everybody at arm's length. Afraid to break the ice. Just stay to yourself, don't extend yourself. See, I know all that shit. I read 'Games People Play' 'bout a dozen times. And I subscribe to 'Psychology Today'. But that's cool, you wanna go through life all closed up and-and-and insular, whatever floats your boat, brotha, I don't give a damn how you live your life. Just want you to know I'm onto you. And I know your fatal flaw, I read you like *that*," and he snapped his fingers, only there was no snapping sound, just a hint of fleshy friction. "Soon as you sat *down!* Wanted *nothin'* to do with me, I could tell. Knew *in*stantly. But like I said, that's alright, 'cause we all got our armor we wear in public, you know what I'm sayin'? You got to protect yourself, I understand that, for whatever reason, whatever demons you're battling, I don't know and I don't care, just know you ain't foolin' nobody... Nobody!"

"Okay," I said.

"That's right…"

"The reason my arms are folded is because I'm cold…"

He waved me off, and muttered, "Don't even waste my time," and walked away.

a generation of leaves

I let you do all the talking because you never listened to anything I said, anyway.

Fortunately, I solved a lot of my problems during your monologues.

Set a lot of goals.

Thought about how I'd eventually leave you during one of your more impassioned soliloquies on the temperature outside.

You never even had a clue.

While you were complaining about how your feet were always cold in the summer and warm in the winter, I was finalizing my plans to leave you the following morning.

What were you thinking when you finally discovered my letter?

You probably sat at the foot of the bed staring at it like a catatonic.

Thinking I was going to come back at five o'clock, fall into your arms, and say, "What-the-hell-was-I-thinking?"

But I didn't.

Thank God.

By that time I was probably smoking in the dining car, drinking that bitter cup of coffee, being hit on by that unctuous little insurance salesman who kept looking down my blouse whenever he thought my eyes were somewhere else.

(Women always know when a guy is checking out her tits, even if she isn't looking at him. Pity you guys never realize that. You just keep on keepin' on with your dumb guy ways).

Kind of like how you never figured out how unhappy I was.

Just kept complaining about George W. or why it took so long for your doctor to mail you the results of your sonogram or why I pay so much for a can of organic pea soup.

Personal choice, I guess.

Seems you've lived your whole life judging others as you judge yourself.

But we all have our own preferences.

Our own style.

We all feel differently.

React differently.

Love differently.

Leave differently.

You never understood that.

Hmm. Too bad.

my humbug

My style is designed to beguile you.

It's a Jackson Pollock painting, a Charlie Parker solo, a Jimmy Hendrix lick, a Tex Avery cartoon.

It has the switch-blade wit of Lenny Bruce, the energy and attitude of a Sex Pistols show.

It's like angry sex with an ex-wife.

It's a junkie's first needle in the morning and that first drink after being off the wagon.

It's your grandmother's kiss when you're sixteen.

It's reading Hunter S. Thompson backwards and upside down.

It should remind you of an acid trip at your aunt's house who's an Evangelical Christian with strong ties to the Tea Party Republicans and reminiscent of picking dandelions in your backyard in the dead of summer and presenting them to your mother who puts them in a drinking glass filled with water and sets them on the window sill in the kitchen above the sink.

I equate it with drinking tequila and smoking hash on a motor boat in the middle of a lake with your buddies during senior skip day as the sun blisters your back until it bleeds.

It's bad poetry and rap performed by Jews for Jesus.

It's a Peggy Noonan speech delivered by Ronald Reagan in front of a rippling flag addressing an audience populated by the Girl Scouts of America during their critical cookie drive.

It's a Buddhist meditation, a Taoist retreat.

It's a placebo prescribed by Dr. Bombay with unintended consequences.

It's Salvador Dali and Norman Rockwell giving birth to a child and that child is me.

It's stream of consciousness.

It's a higher consciousness, an in-and-out of body experience during the High Holy days and it's glad-handing elderly Jewish men with Seagrams on their breath who immediately run back to open their clothing stores the second the Yizkor service begins.

It's pop-up culture and the cigar ashes settling at the bottom of your grandfather's pants pocket, the smell of a rest-room at a drive in movie theater during intermission, the taste of metal in your mouth, the touch of a woman's finger on the nape of your neck as she walks by your desk.

It's a three-hour wait at the motor vehicle department, a dentist's appointment, a rectal exam, a car accident, a lost wallet, a bad haircut, diarrhea, a sudden cold, a pulled neck muscle and a burgeoning pimple on the tip of your nose all in the same day.

It's rejection, dejection, infection, imperfection, vivisection, no inflection, intersection, introspection, detection, election, inspection and catchin' up on the gaps in your education without a tutor in your Tudor home with the two-door garage.

It's contradictions and massive generalizations and holes in your arguments and holes in your underwear and non-sequiturs that have direct connections with things that were previously said.

It's the inner-child, the outer-shell and the soft-meaty part on the belly of a turtle.

It's the Warren Commission on books-on-tape read by the guy who did the voice for Winnie the Pooh.

It's the prequel of an art house film that will have no sequel.

It's righteous indignation followed by anger, denial, repression, suppression, aggression, resignation, forgiveness and acceptance.

It has the hollow ring of truth and is protected by an army of lies.

It's intellectual Barnumism, plagiarizing something in the public domain.

It's pretentious and pedantic and pedestrian, preachy and self-conscious, entertainment for the moron masses as well as a metaphysical feast for tweedy, tenured fern-league professors who cull passages from texts and search for inaccuracies in character delineation, plot structure and the misuse of really big words...

My style may defile you with my bile or it may put you on trial while you travel the miles of tiles and pile on the denials that you file away on that desolate isle somewhere between your smile and your rile.

But it's not meant to be taken literally.

some kind of other

I remember riding on a bus to Natick, Massachusetts to visit a girlfriend. The old lady next to me was verbose. She'd had a few cocktails before boarding. Dewar's Black Label on the rocks. She told me she was "involved in something peculiar," but wouldn't tell me what it was.

Two minutes later, she was reminiscing about her youth and I was starting to yawn.

"Oh, is my life that boring?" the woman said.

I shook my head, said quietly, "No, ma'am..."

I could tell she was looking for an apology from me but I was too tired to give her one.

She droned on. "I used to be a lively young woman who set the world on fire with my effervescence and my joie de vivre... my very, shall we say, promiscuous lifestyle began at Vassar... the exhibitionist side of me, which is, believe me, fairly predominant, was beginning to emerge at the time... my aspirations were to be a good wife to somebody... and then I met this famously open and good-natured and sometimes conscience-troubled and always earnest man..."

Her monologue could have used a few cuts and several revisions, but I wasn't about to become her editor.

I eventually fell asleep against the window and woke up with a headache that required three extra-strength aspirin to relieve the throbbing.

The guy across the aisle from us, dressed all in army fatigues, was smiling at me. "It's all bullshit," he said, giggling like he didn't give a shit about anything.

I looked back at the old lady. She was R.E.M.ing and drooling all over herself. Suddenly she jerked awake and I quickly shut my eyes.

The guy in the fatigues reached over and nudged the old lady. "Hey, your buddy there's fakin' a snooze...I think he's tired of hearin' about the salad days of your life," and he laughed again.

I felt the old lady's eyes on me.

"My father actually did love me," she said. "Didn't know how to say it... and every time I put the pressure on him to try to feel it, to find it in him, he'd dive in deeper away from it..."

I was a little uneasy listening to her reliving all those deep past emotions, but I could tell she had opened a long locked door into a suppressed inner life, so I left her alone.

When we arrived at the bus terminal, I was tired, hungry and irritable. I deboarded, grabbed my bags, went into the terminal and collapsed in the coffee shop.

Forty-five minutes later, I regained consciousness, and was being examined by an HMO-weary emergency room doc with eucalyptus on his breath.

"How are you feeling?" he said.

"Alright."

"You fainted..."

"Wow... I've never done that before..."

"When's the last time you ate?"

"Thursday."

"That's three days ago."

"Yessir. I'm fasting..."

"Ohh... how come?"

"As a religious discipline..."

"Really? Which religion?"

"Gnosticism."

The doc nodded with tremendous uninterest. "I'm going to give you some Ensure. I'd like you to drink two bottles."

"Can't I just go to IHOP?"

I was escorted to the lobby by his nurse, who thanked me and called me hon. "Now you drink that Ensure, now," she said. "It'll help you regain your strength…"

I threw both bottles in the trash. "I've got bad memories of that stuff," I told her. "Is there a phone I can use?"

"There's a payphone outside."

I fished around for some change, but didn't have any. I was going to have to call my girl collect. When the operator asked her if she would accept the charges, my girlfriend said, "I don't think so… not at this point in my life," and hung up. What the fuck, I thought. I just rode 6 hours on a goddamn bus to hear you say, "I don't think so… not at this point in my life?" It didn't make sense. She'd always been a little mercurial, but she'd never not accepted one of my collect phone calls.

I hailed a cab, and told the driver to take me to her apartment.

Pulling into the parking lot, I noticed her car wasn't there. I told the cabbie to wait while I rang the doorbell.

As I approached her apartment, I noticed an envelope taped to the door knocker, addressed to me. I opened it.

There was a typed-written letter inside.

"Dear You Know Who," it began. "We had some good times back then, didn't we? Always drinking champagne in the rain and reciting poems from all those neurotic female poets: Sylvia Plath, Emily Dickinson, and especially Ann Sexton: 'The night I came I danced a circle and was not afraid.' Ooh, la la … Those were most certainly The Days, weren't they?

Did you ever really love me or were you just fooling around with the emotions of my clitoris? I suppose I'll never know. You're gone now. Dead, they say. But I don't believe that for a moment. I think you're living on some commune in Idaho or worshiping the Buddha with some drunken monks up in Vermont or British Columbia or living on a houseboat in the San Diego harbor waiting for the Perfect Storm to bring you out to sea where you can have one final swim with the dolphins. That's how I'd like to remember you, anyway. The truth could be very different, indeed. You might be sleeping alone under a cheap cotton blanket in a men's shelter protecting your valuables from the crackheads and all those other invisible men who gave up the straight and narrow in favor of lying down in the lap of Uncle Sam, waiting to suckle from his big teat. That was never your style, although I did hear you mention your fondness for The Great Society one time during one of your more insane yet lucid moments."

It ended there. She didn't even sign it.

I headed back to the cab and got in.

"Nobody home?" said the cabbie.

I cracked the window. "Uhm, good question," I said, stashing the letter in my pocket.

between eden and the open road

That's where I'll find you.